Salvation

Courtney's Story

The Carpenter Chronicles: Book Three
A Christian Romance

Janice Limb Myers

This is a work of fiction. Names, characters, incidents, and places are either the product of the author's vivid imagination or are used fictitiously. Any resemblance to actual persons either living or dead, business establishments, names, events, and locations is entirely coincidental.

Dedication

For all who seek to know truth. May you
find the door is always open.
Just walk through.

Acknowledgements

A note of thanks to the readers who gave feedback
on this story:
Judy Ard
Sheila Carnegie
Laura Hawkins Hatton
Lynette Anderson

And to Karen Huff for your encouragement.

Chapter One

The more Courtney Carpenter thought about it, the angrier she got. *Stupid Mormon rules*, she thought, throwing her pen down on the table. Pushing her chair back abruptly and rising from her seat, she glared at Grace and Chelsea as if they were monsters responsible for the situation. "That's it! I've had all I can take of this. I'm outta here," Courtney declared firmly as she marched from the room, stomping her feet as she left, just in case they hadn't gotten the message.

"Courtney, wait! Let's talk about this," Grace reached toward her daughter as she stormed off.

Chelsea stared at the empty space that had been so suddenly vacated by her younger sister. "What in the world was that all about?" she asked her mom.

Grace shrugged. "I don't know. She's been disappearing quite a lot recently. Her unexplained outings began shortly after

Carrie and Antonio's engagement party. The closer the wedding gets, the more frequently I see her disappearing acts."

"You're not worried? She's obviously angry about something."

Grace nodded in agreement. "Yes, she is, and I can take a guess at what that might be, but if she wants to talk about it, she'll come to us. Until then, we just have to let her figure things out for herself. She is twenty-three after all. She's a grown woman."

Chelsea sighed. "I guess so, but I just hate to think that my wedding is causing anything but happiness in this family."

Grace placed a hand over Chelsea's. "Don't be silly, darling. You know she's delighted for you and thinks the world of Kade. Whatever it is, it's her own issue."

"But don't you think we should go after her and ask if we can help with whatever it is?"

"Don't let it dampen your spirits. It'll all work out." Now, shall we video call Carrie in New York and make sure she approves of the finished invites?"

Cheered up by the thought of gushing over the wedding plans with her sister, Chelsea nodded and grinned enthusiastically. Since the wedding was to be held in Utah and Carrie was extremely busy with her job as a reporter in New York, she was leaving the family, in particular, Chelsea, to make most of the plans and final decisions for the double wedding. Chelsea loved that her sister trusted her to take care of the finer details of the ceremony and celebration.

"That sounds like a great idea, Mom. I can't wait for her to see what we've done."

* * *

Earlier that day things were going great for Courtney. She sat back in her chair and examined her handiwork. She had no doubt she could have accomplished this task using the computer in probably 30 minutes or less. *Okay, but that's the way other people would have done it*, she thought to herself. *But using the computer could never have created these uniquely charming and graceful invitation envelopes I see spread before me.*

She flipped through the envelopes with pride, admitting to herself that the hand-written envelopes with the extra flourishes and slight imperfections created using her calligraphy pen gave the hand-created look she was hoping for, the look that says, 'We care enough to send the very best.' She chuckled aloud and rolled her eyes as she realized she had just mentally quoted an old Hallmark commercial she'd heard over and over in her youth.

Courtney loaded the finished envelopes into her case and scurried to join her mother, Grace, and sister Chelsea who were sitting at the large dining table in the Carpenter family home stuffing the wedding invitations into the blank inside envelopes. This was the same table where years of memories were created as members of this family – her dad, John, included – joined for family dinners each day at the insistence of her mom. She thought fondly of her adoptive dad who had always been the comedian of the family and kept them in stitches at dinner.

Courtney stopped and closed her eyes for a moment, recalling those days of her youth, still marveling at how this family had adopted her into their home and their hearts at the age of seven.

Chelsea and Grace had taken the day off work today to complete the wedding invitations project while Courtney was taking care of addressing the envelopes. The double wedding of Courtney's two eldest sisters – Carrie and Chelsea - was going to be a joyous occasion. It was a beautiful summer in Utah, and the joint wedding was planned for late August, ensuring the grand reception could be celebrated outdoors on the amazing grounds of the homestead with the mountains as the beautiful, natural backdrop.

Delaying the wedding until August also allowed plenty of time for Carrie and Antonio to make their preparations to come from New York City and for Antonio to meet the requirements to be married in a temple rather than a standard Mormon church used for Sunday worship services and congregational meetings and activities during the week. This was a goal the couple had committed to at the start of their engagement when Antonio had relinquished his role as Prince of Spain.

He had only recently converted and moved from his luxurious lifestyle in a castle in Spain to a flat in Manhattan. He was dedicated to his new religion and planned to follow the tenants of the Church forever. He lived a good Christian life, ensuring he would qualify to take his bride to the temple for their wedding to be sealed to one another for eternity, the fulfillment of both their dreams.

While stuffing the envelopes for mailing, Courtney's mind wandered. *Carrie has found her Prince Charming, literally, and Chelsea is madly in love with hers, and what does that get me? The Little Sister doesn't even get to attend their weddings? How can they do this to me? Everybody will be there except me. What a stupid rule to have to be a member of the church to go inside the temple. I'm never joining that church!*

Her small, elfin features sharpened into anger. She wasn't actually a full sister to the girls; she was technically a first cousin, the daughter of Grace's sister Lucy. When Lucy died and Courtney's father, David, fell into a deep depression, Grace took Courtney into her home, realizing that the drunken stupors David let himself get into every day rendered him incapable of caring for the young girl. When her father's condition only got worse, the Carpenters officially adopted her.

Although Courtney would be eternally grateful for their love and considered herself a part of the family, she was too angry at the circumstances of her life to even consider listening to their teachings on religion and faith. God hadn't been around much for her even when she'd asked for help, or so she thought. After all, He let her mother, and ultimately her father, die. So the young girl felt she had no reason to devote her life to Him, even though the rest of her new family did. She was flat out angry at God, an anger that lasted for years, although the goodness of the Carpenters taking her in and loving her as a member of the family had gradually helped allay that anger.

Anyway, the upshot was that since she was not even a member of the church, she wouldn't be allowed to enter the sacred temple. More importantly, that meant she couldn't attend her own sisters' weddings, which made her mad. Downright mad!

That's what led to the outburst, and storming out of the house, leaving Grace and Chelsea in her wake.

* * *

Courtney retrieved her purse from her bedroom and stormed out of the house, stopping at the entry closet to grab her jacket before realizing, *Duh, it's July for heaven's sake!* Then slamming the front door behind her, she headed down the long, concrete driveway, her thoughts dwelling on the wedding. For the life of her she couldn't understand how a religion could support a God who would keep a family apart at such a special time. *Oh, I get the sanctity and importance of the occasion because I believe that marriage should be for forever, a joining of souls for a lifetime and beyond, but what's the big deal about just walking into a big, beautiful building to see a wedding?*

She felt she couldn't really discuss it with the family and she didn't attend church with them, so she was really frustrated at not being able to think of anyone she could talk with for answers. As she recovered from the loss of her parents as a young child, she made herself at home in the Carpenter household. They had gently tried to introduce her to their religion and their ways, but she had firmly rejected their attempts; the family had eventually backed off and left her alone, feeling she had to live her life whichever way she chose.

However, she couldn't bear the look of hurt and disappointment that would be in their eyes even as they tried patiently to answer her probing and often derogatory questions. No, she needed to talk to someone who was a little more used to having their faith questioned, maybe even torn apart. Rooting in her purse, she dug out her cell phone and scrolled through the list of contacts until she found the one for whom she was searching: Peter Anderson.

She stared at the name as she continued to walk, her pace slowing and her mood lifting as she thought about the man. The Andersons were members of her family's church and lifelong friends of the Carpenters. She had known Peter pretty much since she had come to live here when she was seven years old, and they had become close friends for a while. As they grew, they had lost touch with one another.

Following the death of her uncle and adoptive father, John, the functions and parties at the Carpenter household had trailed off as Grace grieved the loss, so Courtney hadn't seen Peter around as much.

They had kept in touch and made the effort to get together for a while, then he had gone off on his mission to Spain for two years, and that had been that. She recognized him instantly when she saw him for the first time in years at Carrie and Antonio's engagement party a year earlier. She had to admit, the experience had come as quite a shock.

When they had last seen each other in their youth, Peter had been a small, skinny, awkward teenager, not quite sure how to coordinate his limbs or where to put himself in most situations. Unlike herself, who had remained almost waif thin and small, Peter had obviously had a growth spurt in the time they were apart. He was much taller than she was now, his awkward body filled out into a confident representation of perfect manhood.

No longer was he unsure in social situations, he mingled easily and confidently with the crowd that night, his time away obviously working wonders. To top it off, his mission in Madrid had left him with a deep olive tan, his enjoyment of the sun making him darker even than the native Spaniard, Antonio, who stayed out of the sun as much as possible, as was their way.

She had easily spotted the dark brown hair, that contrasted so sharply with her own, in the crowd and began to weave her way through the throng to greet him. Before she had gotten halfway across the floor, he turned, and she caught a glimpse of his face for the first time in a very long time. She remembered stopping in her tracks, being stunned at the transformation in her young teenage friend, now a man.

He had changed so much, except for those eyes. She had dreamed of those eyes many times over the years, and seeing them again had jolted her, frozen her feet to the ground. While hers were like smooth, rich coffee with the merest hint of cream, his were a light, misty grey, a complete and stunning contrast to the dark hair and tanned skin. In her dreams, his eyes swirled with mysticism and wisdom, holding secrets that Courtney could never hope to unravel. Right at that moment, in the gold and red twinkle lights under the night sky, those eyes held everything she had ever imagined they would.

At the same time, they also held familiarity, giving Courtney a sense of belonging, of coming home. The unusual beauty did not detract from the fact that they belonged to her old friend. She had seen them sparkle with mischief, glitter with joy, dull with worry and shine with sympathy.

She had almost forgotten how close the two had been during a very difficult time in her life. He had been there for her, and she had tried to be there for him as he changed from the boy to man-child, struggling with his thoughts and feelings. Along with the sense of joy and comfort, and the surprise reaction to his attractiveness that was causing her heart to beat faster, Courtney also felt guilt. She should have made more of an effort to stay in touch.

As his eyes finally caught hers through the crowd, she raised her hand in a tiny, pathetic wave, her rogue feet having decided to plant deep, strong roots on the spot, holding her firmly in place. She watched as he dodged and weaved his way toward her, casually greeting people here and there, as he eased his way through them, intent on his goal. Finally, he was standing in front of her, his grey suit and deep blue shirt highlighting those smoky eyes.

"Hi," he said simply, his face not smiling, his body still.

"Hi," Courtney replied, her statue-like posture mimicking his.

They held the eye contact, the world around Courtney seeming to fade away as a million and one thoughts raced through her mind. Glimmers of time spent together in the past flashed like a video reel at high speed through her head, every time they had hugged, or she had kissed him on the cheek, or times they had held hands as they ran off to indulge in some childish adventure.

The memory of those touches, so innocent at the time, now brought a flush to her cheeks and her body. Electricity seemed to arc between them, bridging the foot-wide gap. Courtney's wild imagination conjured up images of her as a Faraday experiment, blue sparks and arcs shooting from her every pore, connecting her to Peter in a raw, elemental display of her emotions in turmoil. The burning in her lungs was a sharp reminder that she had forgotten to breathe, but she was powerless to obey the simple requirement her body demanded.

Peter broke into a slow easy smile. "It's good to see you, Courtney," he began with a baritone voice so deep it surprised her. "Nice to see you in a dress for a change."

His reference to her tomboy, childhood self broke the current spell, allowing her to take the deep, rasping breath her body so desperately needed. She was sure she had been on the verge of fainting, although she found the notion completely ridiculous.

This was Peter for goodness sake, her old friend, the one she had played with, rode with, swam with, and built forts with in all their skinny, underdeveloped, immature glory. Teenage tantrums, spotty skin, gawky limbs, they had come through it all together. No wonder they were a little surprised at each other's appearance now.

* * *

Breaking her reverie and images of that long past time, Courtney pushed the button on her phone. Her call was answered after just two rings.

"Hi, Courtney, what's up?"

Since the engagement party, Courtney had made the effort to keep in touch this time, and the two of them had picked up their friendship with ease. She could easily admit to herself that she found him incredibly attractive, but she also knew that a relationship with him was out of the question. She would settle for friendship, and had put some effort into nurturing it under the new parameters, regaining some of the closeness that had come so freely with childhood.

"Hi, Peter. I hope I'm not disturbing you, but I'm pretty riled up about something and need someone to talk to."

"What's wrong?"

The concern in his voice was instant and Courtney felt heartened by it, letting go of some of the anger that had caused her to storm out of the house earlier. If anyone could help her understand and come to terms with what was troubling her, it would be Peter.

"I'm seriously annoyed about not being able to go to the wedding."

"Now's as good a time to talk as any, if you're free. Where are you?"

She knew it. He had instantly understood that she didn't want someone who could magically fix it, but someone who would be a sounding board so she could let her anger out, and would patiently try to help her understand why things were the way they were. As a missionary, he was used to carefully explaining his beliefs and religion, not aggressively defending it or simply quoting from it.

"Walking down the drive," she replied in answer to his question.

"Stormed out in a temper tantrum by any chance?"

Courtney laughed. "How'd you guess?"

"I'll come and get you, I'm leaving right now."

"Can you pick me up at the bottom of the drive? Chelsea is here and if you have to go up to the house to turn, I'll have a million questions to answer when I get back."

"No problem, I'll see you soon."

Chapter Two

"So what you're saying is that the closer someone sticks to the rules, the closer they are to God. The closer they are to God, then the less likely they are to contaminate the inner sanctums and defile the sanctity of the ceremony."

Peter rolled his eyes, puffed out his cheeks and ran his fingers through his hair, leaving it deliciously tousled. "If you want to take everything I have been saying over the past two hours and condense it into the simplest and harshest form you can find, then I guess so."

"But who says these rules are really what God wants from us? Aren't they just an interpretation by some mere mortal? Why am I not a good person just because I like to drink coffee?"

Peter chuckled. "Courtney, you are completely exasperating, do you know that?"

"Well, of course I know that, people have been telling me all my life," Courtney replied with a cheeky grin. "But it doesn't mean my questions are any less serious."

"True, but you know full well that the coffee thing is to do with the fact that we consider our bodies a truly amazing gift, and we try our best not to throw that back in the Creator's face by filling it with harmful substances. It's not about being good or bad; it's about respect and being grateful.

As for interpretations of the rules, then yes and no. They were written by the hand of God, but I guess everyone could read them and see something different in them, as with any other piece of writing, but that's why we have people to guide us in their true meaning.

"Obviously," he continued, "the Bible was written a long time ago, and teaches us about the sacred nature of temples. The ordinances come straight from the Bible. There have been changes required to accommodate certain things that weren't around at the time, or aren't around now, so in a way, they are an interpretation. But in reality, when you truly let God into your heart and your life, you can feel what he wants from you. It's hard to explain, but have you ever had an inner voice nagging at you over something?"

"Sure, I've battled with my conscience on many an occasion when about to reach for that second slice of chocolate cake."

Peter laughed at her again. "Okay, that's as good as anything, I guess, not that you need to watch your figure, you were always a skinny little kid. So when you truly believe that you belong to God, it's a little like that inner voice, the one that knows what is right, despite what anyone or anything else is telling you, be it your head or your tummy. It feels like He is always guiding you, setting you on the right path, and you know instinctively what is right and wrong, whether it's a specific rule or not. So although the rules were written by a person, that person was being guided when he wrote them, and each person who chooses to follow them is being guided by Him, too. Does that make sense?"

Courtney shrugged, fiddling with a button on her casual green top. "I suppose, but I've never experienced it and I'm not sure I want to. I like to be in control, my choices are my own and I live with the consequences for better or worse, and have no one to blame but myself if things go wrong."

"Doesn't that ever get lonely, or too hard?"

"Nope," Courtney declared firmly. "I like being my own woman, and nobody tells me what to do or when to do it. I don't think that makes me unworthy or a bad person. I don't break the law, I don't hurt other people – at least not intentionally, and I live a fairly good life by most peoples' standards. I work hard and earn my place in this world. I still can't see why I would contaminate the precious temple by attending my sisters' wedding. I think it's more to do with secrecy than anything else."

"Our faith isn't about secrecy, it's about sanctity. Have you ever had a dream, an idea or an ambition that you have shared with someone and they have mocked and ridiculed it to the point where it no longer feels special to you, or maybe not even achievable? It's also about salvation, how we can be redeemed from our sins through the atonement of Jesus Christ. He rescues us every day from our sins."

Courtney was startled before she could respond by a sudden light shining in the car window and a swift knock on the glass. They were parked up at one of the local viewpoints that was off the beaten track in the mountains high above Sundance. It had always been one of her favorite spots for soul searching. The beauty inspired her.

Courtney had preferred to stay in the car for the serious discussion, despite Peter's offer of refreshments at the lodge in Sundance. She was startled by the appearance of someone else in the remote spot. Peter turned the key in the ignition and pushed the button to lower the electric window. A face peered in, the flashlight still shining in their eyes. Courtney tried to peer through the beam to identify the face, but Peter solved the puzzle for her.

"Good evening, Officer Bradshaw, how are you this evening?"

"Oh, it's you Peter, I'm good thanks." The officer peered over to the passenger seat. "Courtney," he acknowledged gruffly but tipped the brow of his hat.

"Hi, Officer Bradshaw," Courtney replied politely, disregarding the negative sound in his voice. Everyone knew the local man who helped keep the streets safe. Courtney had known him since she was a child. In fact, he had escorted her home on many an occasion when he considered whatever game she was involved in would lead to mischief and she was "being up to no good" as he used to tell Grace.

"So what are you kids up to parked way up here?"

"Actually, we're having a bit of a theological debate," Peter answered with complete honesty. "Courtney here had some questions about being unable to attend the upcoming nuptials of her sisters at the temple, and I'm trying to help her come to terms with that and understand the reasons."

The officer grunted. "Having any luck with that?"

"Not really," Peter chuckled. "But I intend to keep trying."

Courtney stifled a wry smile. Her staunch anti-organized religion stance while being part of a highly regarded Mormon family had not gone unnoticed or undiscussed among the locals in the small Utah town. Although most accepted her for who she was, some found it shocking and gossip worthy. She had a feeling that Officer Bradshaw might be one of them.

"If it had been anyone else but you, I wouldn't believe a word of that story, Peter. I would assume you were out here neckin'. You're not doing any of that stuff are you?"

Courtney frantically bit her bottom lip while Peter replied in a monotone voice. "No, Officer Bradshaw, no necking."

A small squeak escaped from Courtney. She hadn't heard that term in ages.

"Well, I guess I'd take your word for it more than anyone else's. I'll bid you goodnight. Just make sure you don't get led astray, and don't stay out here too late."

Courtney's suppressed laughter broke free in the form of a snort as the officer straightened up to leave. Peter quickly closed the window, silently urging the policeman to move more quickly out of earshot as Courtney dissolved into helpless giggles beside him. He couldn't help but smile at her mirth, and finally joined her contagious laughter.

"Ohhhh, Peter, I'm such a bad influence on you! You have to be careful around a little temptress like me."

"Well, if anyone could lead me astray, it would be you, Courtney," Peter growled, dropping his head and gazing up at her through thick, black lashes. His grey eyes flashed a steely silver and for a second, Courtney's breath hitched in her throat and time stood still. Then she realized he was teasing her, playing along with the moment.

"Stop it," she cried. "My sides hurt from laughing."

"Okay, back to the serious stuff then," Peter said, grinning at her. "Now, where were we? Oh yes, you were arguing with me again, over the same point we started discussing …" he glanced at the clock on the dashboard, "… two and a half hours ago."

Courtney had the decency to look contrite. "I'm sorry; it's just so frustrating that I can't witness their special moment."

"You'll get to be there for the photographs afterwards, and the ring ceremony at your house, and, of course, the big reception," he said, hoping to console her.

"I know, but it's not the same, is it?"

"I wish there was something I could do, but there just isn't. If special dispensation was allowed for these circumstances you know I would speak for you in a heartbeat, but there isn't such a thing. Even Antonio has been made to wait the full year, and he's one of the grooms."

Courtney giggled again, thinking of Antonio. "That must have been such a shock to you, being asked to teach him about your religion."

"It was. I was taken aback when I was told I needed to see a Catholic who had specifically sought out our teachings, but when I found out it was the heir apparent to the throne of Spain, you could have knocked me over with a feather!"

"Trust Carrie to bag herself a real live prince while following up on a news story. Can you believe that in a few short weeks, the King and Queen of Spain will be right here, in our garden and our home?"

Peter nodded his head. "I know; it sounds crazy doesn't it? And don't forget the new heir apparent, Princess Adelina, will be here too. She's the one that's next in line since Antonio stepped down to be with Carrie, and her older sister is now married to the Prince of Monaco."

"I still can't believe that you were the missionary in Madrid when Antonio contacted the church. What a weird coincidence."

Peter grinned at her. "God works in mysterious ways, and there is no such thing as coincidence."

"You would say that," Courtney laughed, giving him a light, playful punch on the arm.

"Of course I would, because it's true."

"Come on, you'd better get me home before the family sends out a search party. Or even worse … Officer Bradshaw!"

* * *

The cell phone startled Chelsea when it rang so early in the morning. She was awake but sprawled on the bed in her pajamas, her head cushioned by a cluster of pillows, daydreaming about her upcoming wedding and the gorgeous hunk of man she was marrying.

"Hey! How's my favorite twin?" she heard Carter say before she could even utter a greeting.

"Carter, I'm the **only** twin you have!"

"Then that certainly seals the deal; you **are** my most beautiful, kind, loving, understanding and favorite twin!"

"Yah … right! What's up?"

"What's your schedule like today?"

"Today? Are you coming to see us?"

"No, I'd like to come see just *you*."

"Really, how strange. Uh … I'm just working, a few phone calls, and dinner with Kade. You wanna go out with us?"

"No. I'd like to propose a clandestine meeting – just you and me. Don't want anyone else to know about it. Mum's the word! It's early here …"

Chelsea interrupted, "Hey, it's early everywhere! I'm not even out of bed yet."

"Alright, alright. It's early there, too. Could you get away for lunch? I can be at the San Fran airport for a flight in a couple of hours. I'll have to check the flights but I'm sure I can be there before lunch."

"Sure, I can arrange it. This must be something really important if you're flying here just to see me. Got a new gal or something?"

"Can't a guy throw out any surprises anymore? Can't I just miss my twin sister and want to drop in for a nice lunch to catch up on things before she gets married and I'm no longer her favorite man?" It was true that Carter was just that kind of brother. Since he hadn't yet found someone good enough for himself, he often spoiled his sisters with notes, little gifts, time spent together. So this was really not a surprise. They all knew Chelsea was his favorite, although he didn't admit it openly to the others.

So that's it. He's getting a tad worried that Kade will soon be getting all my attention instead of him. "Of course you can! I've got a plan. I've got an easy day today. People are really covering for me so I can work on the wedding. Just text me your flight info when you book it and I'll be at the Salt Lake Airport to pick you up. Then we can spend whatever time we can, run around, have lunch or something. Are you thinking of dropping into the CGP office and surprising Mom and Courtney?"

"Well, I thought it could just be a twin day before your wedding. I think that surprise will have to wait for another day. I've got some pressing business that only allows me a few hours to spend with the best friend a guy ever had."

"Wow! You're sure in a sentimental mood today."

He laughed. "I'll text you as soon as I have the flights booked."

"Okay, I'll see you at the airport. I'll just park out front and wait there."

"Thanks, Sis. Love ya. Bye."

"Me, too. Bye."

Chelsea found she was so excited to see Carter she'd already gotten up and started making her bed before the call ended. *Gosh I miss him! This is going to be a fun day.*

And it was. They talked, they laughed. Just like old times when Maggie would fix them a lunch basket and they'd ride out on their horses to sit under their favorite shade tree and eat lunch. And share secrets.

This day wasn't much different. Carter had surprised Chelsea with a new love interest in his life, a woman who had lived a very different life than the Carpenters, but whom he thought was likely to steal his heart away. He was beaming! Sharing the news with Chelsea first had always been a great way of gauging how the rest of the family would take the news.

When Chelsea dropped him off at the airport for his return flight, Carter was relieved and confident the rest of the family would be accepting, too. He'd tell them about Kate when he returned to Utah for the wedding.

"Remember, mum's the word," he said to Chelsea as he gave her a quick kiss on the cheek and opened the car door. "We'll break the news to the family in a couple of weeks."

Chelsea grinned and blew a kiss as he turned to go through the sliding doors to catch his plane.

Just like old times. Carter and I have a secret. Though she could never have imagined just how that secret was going to impact the lives of the entire Carpenter clan.

Chapter Three

Courtney was interrupted in reading a manuscript by the knock on her office door. She scowled at the intrusion but her face relaxed slightly as her sister popped her head through the door.

"Do you have five minutes?" Chelsea asked.

"For you, I suppose so," she replied ungraciously. She already suspected that this impromptu visit had more to do with wedding plans than the Carpenter's family-owned publishing business that employed them both.

Chelsea came into the room and took a seat across the desk from Courtney. She glanced at the manuscript Courtney had been reading and noticed she had used a finger to mark her place. "Anything exciting?"

"Actually, yes, thrilling. This is the first draft of Antonio and Cassie's maiden collaboration." Cassie, the experienced novelist of the family with multiple best-sellers under her belt connected with Antonio when they first met in Utah for the engagement party. Carrie suggested the two could collaborate on a novel as a way of assisting Antonio in getting started in his writing career, and a partnership was born. Cassie and Antonio immediately set out to create their first book together and submit it to Courtney for publication by Carpenter Global Press.

Chelsea almost squealed in excitement. "How is it?"

"So far so good, really good actually. I think we might end up with three authors in the family, two sisters and a brother-in-law."

"That's great news. Have you told Carrie yet?"

"No, not yet. I wanted to read the whole thing before I gave her my honest opinion."

"Good call. Anyway, I can see that you're itching to get back to it and I don't blame you. I'll make this quick. I have an appointment booked at Sweet Sensations tomorrow afternoon for cake tastings and I was hoping you would come with me."

"Isn't Kade going with you?"

"He was going to, but he's been called to a meeting, one that Mom is also attending, before you ask."

"So I'm third choice?" Courtney asked huffily, her continuing discouragement about her place in the family becoming more evident.

"No, I wanted you to come anyway, but now it will just be the two of us instead of the four."

"I'm just not into all this wedding stuff, Chelsea," Courtney sighed, marking her place in the manuscript with a pencil and removing her finger so she could run her hands through her hair.

Chelsea looked hurt. "Won't you tell me what's wrong? I know something is, but I can't figure it out. Is it because you're going to be working alongside your brother-in law? Does that seem awkward for you?"

"That's got nothing to do with it. Besides, you know I want to head up a branch somewhere else as soon as Grace thinks I'm experienced enough. If I have my way, and I usually do, I won't be in Utah much longer."

Chelsea nodded, acknowledging the truth of her words; Courtney usually did get what she wanted. "So what is it then?"

Courtney could read the hurt in her sister's eyes and she crumbled, unwilling to let Chelsea come to her own conclusions. She sighed deeply before she finally confessed what was upsetting her about this whole thing. "It's this stupid forbidden Mormon temple rubbish. I can't believe two of my three sisters are getting married in a joint ceremony, and I'm the only member of our family who isn't even allowed in the door."

Relief flooded Chelsea's face. "Oh, thank goodness that's all it is."

"All? You call that 'all'?"

"Please don't be mad at me, it's just that I've been imagining all sorts of things that led me to believe that gaining a husband would somehow cause me to lose a sister. You know I couldn't bear that."

Guilt flooded through Courtney as she realized her bad attitude about the wedding and keeping quiet about her reasons had such a detrimental effect on her sister. Chelsea had enough to worry about right now as it was.

"Why didn't you mention it before?" Chelsea asked her gently.

"I didn't want to start any religious arguments in the family. You know we live and let live, but this has been eating me up. I want to be there so much."

"I understand, and in this instance, I wish it could be different, too, but it is what it is, and we're having the ring ceremony afterward especially for you and Antonio's family. Courtney, can I tell you something?"

"Sure, you know you can talk to me about anything."

"With Carrie and Antonio living in New York and leaving everything up to me, I'm having a really hard time. Planning your own wedding is stressful enough, even with all the help that the family fortune can provide. But having to choose things and make decisions for other people is a nightmare. It's Carrie's very special day too, and I'm terrified I'll mess things up for her. I could really use your help and support. I know you have great taste and having someone to back me up on whether Carrie will be happy would mean so much to me. Will you help me?"

Courtney completely melted at her sister's heartfelt plea. "Of course I will, and I'm sorry I've been such a grouch about this whole thing. I'll be finished with this manuscript by the end of the day today. I have to admit I'm shocked you've left cakes this late. You don't need a baker; you need a magician!" Seeing her sister's crestfallen face, she quickly changed her tactics. "What time are we leaving tomorrow to stuff our faces with cake then?"

Chelsea's face brightened and the girls laughed, relieved that the tension that had been building between them was now broken. They finalized their schedule for the following day and Courtney watched Chelsea practically skip out of her office. She smiled and shook her head. *Brides,* she thought, *completely loopy.*

* * *

Courtney immersed herself in helping with the wedding plans as much as she possibly could, being the best sister she could be. As time ticked by and the event grew closer, her life seemed to be a flurry of work and meetings, finalizing menus, cakes, flowers, favors, gifts; the list seemed endless. Grace had told Chelsea at the beginning she should hire a wedding planner to do all the hard work for her, but Chelsea had insisted on the more personal touch, wanting to choose things individually for her and her eldest sister.

Although hundreds of staff would be employed on the day for the ring ceremony and the reception that would be held on the beautiful grounds of the family estate, Chelsea had elected to do all the legwork herself. Courtney was exhausted and she wasn't even in the wedding party.

Still, she had to admit that being this involved in the planning and preparation was helping her to feel more a part of the big day, even though she would miss the actual ceremony itself.

Carrie and Antonio arrived at the family estate with far less fanfare than provided for their engagement party. After all, back then it was a really big deal as none of the family members had met Antonio, although they'd certainly seen him on television with his public announcement of his love for an American journalist. And they were all so eager to meet a member of the Royal Family of Spain.

Now Antonio was living in New York City in an apartment not far from Carrie's. Her work schedule was sometimes erratic as newspaper work often is, and she was still traveling to Europe on assignments. Her success in covering the oil tanker crisis in Spain had seen to that.

Antonio was trying his hand at being an author and was collaborating with Cassie, Carrie's younger sister, on his first novel which had now been submitted to Carpenter Global Press for possible publication. He wrote like there was no tomorrow while Carrie was traveling to ensure they had plenty of time to spend on their relationship when she was home.

The family was there to greet them when they arrived at the estate in Midway. Maggie planned a special dinner for the group, and Carter asked for a family meeting after dinner. For the first time this would include both the soon-to-be spouses of his sisters and every member of the family was requested to be in attendance.

Everyone arrived on time - Grace, Carrie and Antonio, Chelsea and Kade, Carter, Cassie - except Courtney, who once again was out with Peter. Grace decided to go ahead with dinner without Courtney so Maggie could get out of the kitchen, and have the family meeting afterward. But they wanted Courtney to join in the meeting and most figured she probably had forgotten, being distracted these days by Peter.

"I'll give Courtney a call to remind her," Cassie offered so she can be here when we're all finished with dinner.

"Great!" was the unison reply from the group. Courtney was no less a member of this family than any of them were. There was only a vague recollection of the sad child who had joined their family sixteen years before.

Grace stood and the others followed suit as she added, "Then let's all head to the dining room. It smells, terrific! Save me a place and I'll check on Maggie." Everyone chuckled at that since Grace always sat in the same chair she had sat in since she and John built the house so many years ago, even before most of them were born.

"I'll be right there. Just calling Courtney now." Cassie punched in a '6' on her speed dial and waited for Courtney to answer, but the ringing continued until the voice mail picked up. "Hey, Court! We're just sitting down to dinner and I wanted to remind you we'll be waiting for you to come home for the family meeting when dinner is over. Oh, and don't forget, it's family only, so you'll have to say goodnight to that hunk. I think Carter may have a pretty important announcement to make, so get on home, will you? See you soon!"

She hung up wondering why Courtney wouldn't answer her call. Maybe things are going so great with Peter she doesn't want any interruptions. She decided to go ahead and send a text message as well just to be sure. She typed into the keyboard:

"Sitting down to dinner. Come home for family-only meeting. Something's up. Carter's acting strange. We 're waiting for you."

Well, I guess that's the best I can do right now. She put her phone in her pocket and went into see what seat was left in the dining room. She didn't care where she sat. "Let's eat ... I'm famished!"

"Did you get her?" Chelsea asked?

"No. Left a voice mail and sent a text. This thing with Peter must be getting pretty serious."

She took the remaining chair, Grace asked Kade to offer the blessing on the food, and everybody dug in to eat while lively conversations continued around the table.

It wasn't long before Cassie's phone buzzed. She grabbed it and read, "Got it. On my way home."

"Courtney got the message; she's on her way home." A chorus of cheers rang out. The Carpenter family is strong and united. Even though they live from coast to coast, when one has news, they all want to share it. Carter was most relieved to hear Courtney was on her way so the entire family would be here for his news. Truth be told, he was a bit nervous about how everyone would feel about his new love. She didn't fit the Carpenter mold.

"Hey, guys!" Courtney yelled as she entered the back door. She followed her nose through the kitchen and into the dining room, then walked around the table welcoming everybody home with a hug and a kiss. "What's up?"

"I think everyone's finished, so let's go ahead and take a break if you need it and we'll gather in the family room and turn the evening over to Carter. Deal?"

"Deal!" echoed through the room as everyone got moving, some to the family room, others to find a bathroom in advance of an expected long meeting. They had so much to talk about before the weddings.

When everyone was refreshed and seated in the family room, they all looked toward Carter who took his cue to begin. This was nothing new for Carter; he had been leading family meetings since his father, John, had died on a ski slope in Park City.

"Thank you all for being here. It's so great to come home and have everybody here. Thanks for showing up, Courtney," he teased. "And we welcome our new family members, Antonio and Kade. Your wives have instructed me that I'm not to scare you off tonight." Everyone chuckled.

Carter continued. "Maybe this is becoming yet another tradition in the Carpenter household. Chelsea and Kade started it to announce their engagement since, of course, Carrie and Antonio had already made their announcement in front of the world on international T.V." Everyone laughed as Antonio jumped to his feet, pulled Carrie beside him, and took a very overstated bow. Grace felt so happy that Antonio now fit right in with the rest of her children.

"I'm just going to throw this out to you," he continued. "This is not, I repeat not, an engagement announcement." Rowdy shouts of disappointment could be heard around the room, making Carter laugh.

"Okay, here it is without the drama. I've met someone."

"*Met* someone?" Cassie interjected while Carter rolled his eyes.

"Okay, I'm in love. Does that sound better, Cassie? I'd better not see this in your next novel," he pretended to scold. They all often wondered if their escapades would turn up in one of

Cassie's stories. And now they had Antonio, the author, to worry about too.

"Oh, yah. Now you're talkin' Bro!" Once again laughter filled the room. Carter figured he'd better get this out quickly before he was teased to death.

"Look," he continued, "Kate's not exactly the girl you all may be hoping for, so I wanted to warn you before I 'bring her home to meet mom,' so to speak." Now he held their attention.

"I met Kate at school in California. In fact, she was Josh's girlfriend. Oh, for you newest members of the family, Josh was one of my best friends and my roommate in college, so Kate was over at our place all the time and we did a lot of fun things together, just the three of us or on double dates. But then I went off to graduate school at Colombia and lost track of them. Kate and Josh married and had one son, a really cute little blond-headed kid.

"I ran into Kate one day in San Francisco, about six weeks ago. Josh had recently died" … Carter had decided not to mention the suicide … "so she and her son were on their own to run the winery Josh had started. I've tried to help her out and, well, the friendship was quickly renewed and things went forward from there. It's not the usual Carpenter romance, although I've come to believe there isn't a 'usual' Carpenter romance."

"You've got that right," Courtney chimed in to the laughter of her siblings.

"I just wanted you to know about Kate and my desire to help her adjust to being a widow, a single mom, and the operator of a winery all at once. We're a couple now and I think in time, if I'm lucky enough, we'll be more than that … maybe even an unconventional family by Carpenter standards.

"I hope to bring her home to meet all of you as soon as she and Josh can get away. And, I guess, that's about all I have to say on the matter."

"Oh, no!" Carrie interjected as Carter sat down. "You're not getting off that easy. Tell us all about her. Where's she from? What does she look like? How old is her son?"

And as was the custom in the Carpenter household, the night wore on with discussions and frivolity until everyone was worn out.

Later that night Antonio and Kade took their leave, Kade returning to his apartment and Antonio driving up to the rented house in Sundance for the night. The Carpenter clan settled in to their childhood rooms at the homestead for the night, each feeling loved and very grateful for their forever family.

* * *

Despite being far happier now that she understood the reasons she couldn't go into the temple for the weddings, Courtney hadn't given up her meetings with Peter to discuss the issue. She knew she was using it as an excuse now just to see him, but she did genuinely have many questions regarding his faith. He told her that he missed being a missionary and was glad of the opportunity to teach her, even if he knew her soul was lost a long time ago. Courtney chuckled ruefully. He was speaking tongue-in-cheek when he'd said it, but she couldn't help but wonder if he really felt that way about her. Was it true? Was she really lost?

She didn't feel that way. She knew she was loved, she knew who she was, and she knew what she wanted. At least she thought she did. Her plan was set long ago: great grades at high school, graduate from the University of Utah, go straight to work in the family firm, prove her ability and trustworthiness to Grace.

Once that had been accomplished, she would beg for a transfer and a promotion, in the hope of heading up a branch office somewhere in a much more vibrant and exciting city, like New York or San Francisco, maybe even overseas one day. Carpenter Global Press was as global as the name suggested. They had branches and affiliates all over the world. It could be hers for the taking and she knew she was well on the way to fulfilling her dreams.

Just now, though, it didn't seem so pressing; she found herself not in quite as big a hurry to leave the confines of her family and Utah.

Her sudden change of heart came as a surprise to her, and she grappled through her mind to figure out the train of thought that led to that shocking discovery. She'd been looking in her diary for appointments, wondering if there were more wedding-related items to be dealt with after work or during her lunch hour today.

Thinking about the wedding made her think of Peter and then … *Oh crap, that was it!* Courtney groaned as she realized her procrastination about leaving Utah stemmed from the fact that Peter was back. She knew the minute she saw him again that she was attracted to him, and that they were rekindling the deep, close connection they'd shared as childhood friends, but she hadn't taken the time to consider that her feelings were running far deeper than that.

"Well, that's just downright silly and idiotic and pointless and futile and any other dang word you can think of!" she told herself firmly in a much louder voice than intended.

She jumped as her assistant knocked and popped her head in the door. "Did you call me, Courtney?"

"Umm, no."

"Sorry, I thought I heard you shout out loud. Apologies for the interruption then," June stammered, looking confused as she ducked back out the door and closed it behind her.

Courtney shook her head, reprimanding herself. June's appearance soundly reminded her that she was at work, and she'd better knuckle down and get on with it.

As the day was nearing a close, she picked up her cell phone and texted Peter, asking if he had plans that evening. His reply that he was free brought a grin to her face. Her thumbs flying, she asked if he would care to meet her at the diner they both loved in Midway and his enthusiastic response only made her smile grow wider.

She came up with a brilliant plan. *I'm not the girl for him. Obviously he loves and respects his religion and has never even considered someone outside his faith. That means he's got to find a relationship with someone who feels exactly the same about it. And that girl is definitely not me, so whatever these feelings going on here are, they certainly are an unwelcome and unwanted inconvenience. Get over it, Girl.*

She would treat it like a phobia, using the desensitization technique. She would overload her senses with him as much as possible, talking on the phone, spending as much time together as possible, texting, emailing and any other contact she could come up with. She would do this until the excitement and thrill of being with him turned to familiarity, getting to the point where the thought of seeing him no longer gave her butterflies, when his warm laugh didn't tie her tummy in knots and when his smile didn't cause her heart to stutter. It was genius! She knew it would be hard initially, but she was strong and determined; she would get there. *Yes, you can do this!*

* * *

Sitting in the booth across from Peter as he reached over and wiped a small smear of ketchup from the corner of her mouth, she began to doubt that strength and resolve she believed in earlier. He looked positively edible in his khaki shirt and pale blue jeans, even more so than the burger and fries sitting in front of her. He obviously took time to go home and change from his office attire before meeting her.

Since his return from his mission, he worked at his father's law firm and she expected him to arrive in his suit and tie. He looked gorgeous in suits, but she had to admit the casual look was divine on him, too. As he spoke, she found herself watching that full, firm mouth move rather than listening to the words. She stared at him, lost in a fantasy about what she would like to be doing with that mouth, thinking there were far better ways to occupy it than talking or eating.

"Earth to Courtney, Earth to Courtney. Hello?"

"Uh, what? Did you say something?"

She shivered as he laughed that slow, easy laugh, the one that was so sexy it practically made her toes curl.

"I asked how the wedding plans were going."

"Oh, right. Everything's come together just fine, which is just as well considering there's only a week to go. Carrie and Antonio will be arriving this weekend, then his family will follow, arriving from Spain two days or so before the big event."

"That's got to be exciting. Are they staying at your place?"

"No," Courtney shook her head then popped a fry in her mouth, chewing carefully before completing her answer. "Carrie's staying with us, of course, but the family has booked one of the rental houses in the mountains at Sundown."

"Wow, isn't that a bit ... rustic ... for Royalty?"

"That's what I said, but the place is stunning, with luxurious furnishings," she grinned, waving a fry in the air. "Besides, Antonio has assured us they are looking forward to it tremendously. They can't wait to be just another set of tourists, away from the formality and ceremony of their lives. They're hoping for everything to be strictly low key, no press, no staff, no bodyguards, and be just normal people attending their son's wedding and enjoying a vacation. From what they told us, it's just as well that the oldest sister isn't coming; apparently she'd be horrified at having to fend for herself without a cadre of maids to wait on her."

Courtney's eyes glinted mischievously with the gossip, waiting for Peter's reaction.

"Why's that, is she a bit of a spoiled brat?"

Courtney's laugh tinkled out over the busy diner. "Well, he didn't put it quite like that." She lowered her voice. "He said she had taken a little too well to the easy life of being waited on and enjoyed the public adoration too much, possibly not for the right reasons."

"Just as I said, a spoiled brat."

"Oh, harsh!" Courtney joked. "Anyway, she's not coming so it doesn't matter. According to Carrie, the younger sister is delightful."

"Yes, I had the honor of meeting Princess Adelina on several occasions and she truly is a joy to be around. You're going to love her."

"Of course, I almost forgot that you'd spent a huge amount of time at the Royal Palace teaching Antonio in Madrid. Did you meet the king and queen?"

Peter hastily swallowed a mouthful of food before answering. "Eventually, yes, I met them both."

"What are they like?" Courtney leaned toward him, anxious for anything that would give her an idea of what to expect from the Royal Family of Spain.

Peter leaned back, chewing slowly while he considered his answer. "King Benito is quiet, reserved really. He has a great booming voice when he does speak, but he's very pleasant and gentle underneath. Queen Isabella is more forceful and outright, but she's a darling. There's quite a wry sense of humor under her prickly shell."

"Didn't Carrie have a bit of a run in with her?"

"Well, yes, I guess you could call it that. Isabella warned Carrie off, told her to leave her son alone for the good of Antonio and Spain."

"That's mean," Courtney said, her mouth turning down, her brows furrowed, putting on her little pouty act.

"Not really. He was the heir apparent, and set to take over the throne in less than a year. Isabella didn't know the depth of feelings they shared with each other; she thought it was just a silly, embarrassing fling. And she didn't know anything about Carrie except she was a journalist and an American. Two strikes against her! Journalists don't really have the best of reputations in Spain and the way many of them treated Spain covering the recent oil spill didn't help.

"All Isabella knew was that the press would have a field day with Antonio being involved with an American journalist. It would damage his reputation and the standing of their family tremendously once it got out. She soon came around once Antonio actually sat down and talked to them both.

"By then she knew how in love he was and could see how miserable it left him to be without Carrie when she was back in

New York. She wanted to make right what she had done to Carrie and was in on the plan for that very public declaration of Antonio's love."

Courtney grinned. "I guess I should thank her then, because that televised declaration and proposal was something I wouldn't have missed for the world and without her interference, it wouldn't have happened. I'll never forget the shock on Carrie's face, her expression was priceless!"

"It certainly was a memorable moment. I was there in the crowd with the rest of Madrid. Can you imagine how surprised I was to hear Antonio say the name of my neighbor, Carrie Carpenter, back home?"

"Tell me more about your time in Spain."

The two continued to talk and eat, Courtney fascinated by Peter's missionary days but at the same time longing for her plan to work, and work quickly.

Chapter Four

Shocked out of a sound sleep by an alarm clock that went off earlier than usual, Courtney frowned in confusion as she opened her eyes to see the rising dawn. She leapt out of bed as reality filtered through her sleep-fuddled brain. *Today's the wedding day!* She threw on some casual clothes, knowing she would be showering and dressing later, and dashed to the window to check out the sounds already emanating from the yard below.

Despite the early hour, trucks were already arriving and people scurrying over the grounds, setting up marquees, dance floors, erecting stages and running electrics. The grounds were naturally beautiful, but within a few hours, they would be transformed into a magical wonderland fit for two beautiful brides.

Thinking of how the kitchen would soon be commandeered by the caterers, she rushed downstairs to grab some coffee before she would be in the way.

Entering the large work area, she found Maggie, the housekeeper and cook with her daughter Simone, fussing over preparations.

"Hey Maggie, you're off this weekend, remember," she grinned, knowing full well that the housekeeper wouldn't trust anyone else with the arrangements and would have to oversee things, even though she was supposed to be a just a guest today.

Maggie grinned back at her. "I put the coffee on, just for today."

Courtney gave her a hug. No one else drank coffee, it was forbidden in the Mormon faith so Courtney was usually on her own in its preparation. Years ago, when Grace still had hopes of bringing Courtney around, she banned Maggie from "encouraging her" and told her not to buy or make coffee. It hadn't stopped Courtney; she merely bought it and made it for herself.

Courtney turned to Simone and gave her a hug. "It feels like I haven't seen you in ages. How are you?"

Simone was a few years older than the Carpenter girls and had been a bit of a wild child too. At fourteen, she ran away from home to be with some deadbeat guy who was already twenty-one. She lied about her age to get waitressing work, and it was two years before she spoke with her mother again. It all happened just after Maggie and her husband, Nigel, had come to work for the Carpenters, settling into the cute little cottage built to house the caregivers on the estate grounds.

By the time the Carpenter kids were around, Simone was fully reconciled with her family and was with them at the cottage frequently, helping her mother with special functions or just visiting for the weekend. She was as much a part of the family now as were Maggie and Nigel.

"I'm good, thanks. It's great to see you too. I'm sorry I haven't been back since the engagement party, but guess what? I've started doing some classes at UVU in Orem."

"That's great, Simone! So you're going for your GED?"

"Been there; done that! And, yes, I was an idiot dropping out of high school the way I did, but I've got dreams too, and the GED was only the first step."

Courtney poured herself a cup of her black, liquid gold and turned back to Simone. "This seems to be a great day for dreams coming true, tell me yours."

"If I can get the grades and manage to pass the LSAT, I want to go on to study law. My dream is to attend the Clark School of Law at BYU, but I hear it's really hard to get accepted. I know it's going to take years, and it's a huge leap from waitress to practicing law, but if I'm patient and hardworking, I can do it, and maybe even graduate before retirement age."

Simone laughed regretfully, knowing how much time she had wasted in her precious life.

Courtney laid down her mug and rushed in to give Simone another hug. "You *will* do it; I have no doubt. We girls can do anything we set our minds to. If ever you're faltering or doubting yourself, you come to me, got it?"

Simone nodded, her eyes glistening with unshed tears.

"Now, if you'll excuse me, I think I have a bride to assist this morning!"

Courtney downed the rest of the mug and refilled it from the pot, taking it with her as she hurried from the room. Bounding up the stairs, balancing the cup of coffee with practiced ease, she didn't spill a drop. She listened carefully at Chelsea's childhood bedroom door, checking for sounds of movement before she knocked. She didn't want to wake her up if she was still sleeping, but she had a feeling sleep might have evaded her sister the night before. Hearing noises that confirmed movement inside the room, she knocked gently and waited for the soft voice to call to her to come in.

Chelsea was sitting at her dressing table, staring in despair at her reflection in the mirror. She turned to Courtney as she entered. "I couldn't sleep a wink last night, look at me, I look terrible!"

"No, you don't, you look as beautiful as ever," Courtney replied gently as she walked over to her sister, resting one hip on the side of the dresser. *Here's where I earn my big pay check!*

"No, I don't," Chelsea wailed. "My eyes are bloodshot and feel all gritty and I'm all puffy and swollen. I could pack these bags under my eyes for my honeymoon! That's if Kade even still wants to go ahead with it after he catches sight of me today."

Courtney giggled at her sister's histrionics. "Kade would marry you even if you turned up at the temple in your nightgown and ratty old slippers with curlers in your hair," she reassured Chelsea, giving her a playful nudge. "Now, let me see."

She set her mug down on the dresser and gently lifted her sister's chin, turned her face from side to side, pretending to look for the invisible imperfections that Chelsea perceived in the mirror. Playing along, knowing it was the only way to calm her down, she nodded thoughtfully.

"Okay, I don't think it's anything that fifteen minutes can't solve, and we have plenty of time. Lie down on the bed, relax, and I'll be back in a jiffy."

Courtney flew back down the stairs taking them two at a time. Barreling into the kitchen, she dashed for the fridge and hunted around until she found what she was looking for. Triumphantly she held up a cucumber to an amused Maggie and Simone, who were still working in the kitchen. Maggie raised a questioning eyebrow at her.

"Lack of sleep crisis with wedding day jitters inducing paranoid tendencies," Courtney explained.

"Puffy eyes?" Maggie asked.

"Yep, you got it, or so she thinks anyway!"

"Cold, used tea bags are great for that … oh, of course you won't have any," Simone added, flushing as she realized her error.

"No, they don't, and I hope you don't either." Maddie gave her daughter a stern look. Rejoining the religion and atoning for her earlier mistakes was a large part of Simone's turn around in life. "Remember, you're walking into a temple later on today," she teased.

"Don't worry, Mom, I haven't been cheating because I'd only be cheating myself."

Courtney angrily sliced at the cucumber with the largest knife she could find, annoyed at the turn the conversation had taken. Right now was not a good time to be reminded of her so-called shortcomings.

Sweeping the slices off the chopping board and onto a side plate, she bounded back upstairs, where Chelsea had obeyed her orders and was lying on the top of her covers, wrapped in her white fleecy robe, swaddled in pillows. *That girl knows how to follow instructions!* Laying the saucer next to her coffee mug, Courtney dashed to her mother's room, where she knocked on the door before popping her head in.

"Oh good, you're up," she smiled to Grace, who sat on the bench at the end of her bed fully dressed.

"Yes, just bracing myself for the chaos that is about to begin," Grace laughed. "How are things in Camp Chelsea?"

The girls had devised a plan for the morning. Courtney would help Chelsea, while Cassie helped Carrie with all her preparations, allowing Grace to room hop, spending equal time with each of the girls. Once the brides were almost ready, the others would dash off to get themselves ready before returning to help the brides into their traveling clothes, the final touch.

In order to involve Courtney more, the sisters decided they would wear their travel outfits to the temple, change into their wedding gowns in the brides' room, and wear the gowns for photographs at the temple after the ceremony and traveling home for the ring ceremony. Courtney was touched by their gesture to include her as much as possible.

"Not so good at the moment, she didn't sleep too well," Courtney answered. Seeing the look of concern that crossed Grace's face, she quickly expanded. "Just excitement, nothing else, and I've got it under control. Can I raid your bathroom cabinets?"

"Of course you can, help yourself to anything you need. I'm not sure if Cassie's awake yet so I'm going to go to the guesthouse to check on her and be sure Carrie's awake. I'll be in within the hour."

"Great," Courtney cried from the *en suite*, already rummaging through the contents. Locating facemasks, she opened one lid and sniffed. *Too sweet and relaxing*, she thought. *I need something invigorating.* Reading the labels of a few others, she found what she was looking for in a sumptuous and expensive looking brand. Taking another sniff, she smiled. *Perfect!*

Rushing back through to Chelsea's bedroom, she reassured her sister while she applied the luxurious face mask then placed a slice of chilled cucumber over each of her eyes, eliciting a huge sigh from Chelsea.

"Am I allowed to talk?" Chelsea giggled, feeling much more relaxed now that someone else was in charge.

"You can talk only if you're careful not to crack the mask," Courtney replied with mock severity.

"In fifteen minutes, you'll look like you've enjoyed a great night's sleep."

"Okay, I promise. I wanted to ask you something,"

Courtney could hear the trepidation in her sister's voice, and wondered where this was leading. "Sure, go ahead," she said casually.

"I just wondered if you could maybe give me some advice, you know, about what to expect."

Courtney looked confused. "I haven't got a clue, Chelsea, I've never been inside a church never mind a temple, but I imagine it would be like any other wedding ceremony won't it?"

"Oh, I didn't mean about the ceremony, I meant about" … she paused … "tonight."

"Oh, come on, Chelsea, you've been attending parties and receptions all your life. The only difference is that you'll be the one to have to cut the cake and dance a few special dances, that's it. You don't even have to make any speeches, that's up to Kade and Antonio and their best men. Everything's going to be fine."

"Oh, dear," Chelsea replied. Her face screwed up and she began wringing her hands.

"Watch that mask!" Courtney said. "Come on then, out with what's bothering you. It's only you and me, say what it is you really want to say or we'll be at this guessing game all morning."

She watched her sister swallow hard. "Okay, I wanted to ask you about tonight, you know, the *wedding* night."

Courtney frowned in annoyance as she suddenly realized what Chelsea was trying to ask. "You took Biology 101, too. You know where everything goes."

Chelsea sighed deeply. "I know the logistics of it, yes. I was hoping for a more personal take on it, things like how to be sexy, what to expect to feel, if it will hurt, that kind of thing."

Courtney's scowl deepened further and she was glad that Chelsea's eyes were covered. She absently retrieved an excess slice of cucumber and nibbled on it as she tried to contain her laughter.

"What makes you think I can tell you any of that?"

Chelsea's head whirled in Courtney's direction as the cucumber slices lifted as the eyebrows beneath shot upward. Chelsea sat up with a start, flinging the cucumbers slices to the floor.

"Oh, Courtney, I'm so sorry! I've misjudged this completely haven't I? It's just that you dated so much in high school and college, and you went out with Tom for such a long time, I just assumed ..." her voice fell away, the despair at her incorrect assumptions apparent in the ending wail.

Courtney considered her words. *There's no denying I've dated a lot. I'd even concede that I began dating quite young, far younger than Grace had been happy about once she found out.*

Her early dates had an air of innocence about them, hands held under booths at the diner as they hung out there in groups, an arm around the shoulders in the movie theatre, maybe even a stolen chaste kiss before parting. Her later dates had been more adventurous, including beer downed at football games, and make-out sessions in cars parked at secluded viewpoints.

The thing was she never felt any of those sensual feelings when indulging in physical contact with her boyfriends, not even Tom. It wasn't that she considered her virginity anything special or something to be valued, she just hadn't ever felt turned on by them the way she thought she should be. So she'd felt there was no point in going any further with any of them.

The fact that other people made the same assumption about Courtney as her sister just did had saved Courtney from teasing, or even ridicule by her peers in high school and college.

Thinking it all over, she decided it was probably unfair of her to be angry with Chelsea for her assumption. In a much gentler tone, she attempted to put her at ease.

"I'm sorry, Chelsea, I've never gone all the way either, it's Mom you need to ask."

"Ewwww, no way!" Chelsea squealed, restoring the good humor of the room. "I guess we'll just have to fumble our way through, since it'll be the first time for both of us."

"I'm sure you'll both have a *lot* of fun finding out together," Courtney said suggestively, poking her sister and causing her to squeal and giggle again.

Just at that moment, Grace popped her head inside the door. "What's going on in here?" she asked as she stepped into the room.

"Nothing!" the girls replied in unison, then fell onto the bed in laughter.

Chapter Five

With everyone now ready, Courtney rushed to the bottom of the stairs to stand with Cassie, Grace, Maddie and Simone in order to see the full effect of the brides as they stepped out onto the top landing. She gasped as they appeared together and stood at the top of the stairs, hand in hand.

Carrie's outfit was reminiscent of the Audrey Hepburn era, a beautiful satin shift dress in rich cream that ended at exactly half way between knee length and calf length. The dress was paired with a bolero jacket with full-length sleeves, the whole outfit demure and proper, yet sexily feminine in its innocence.

Chelsea's suit was of the purest linen, the dress ending just below the knee, and the soft, flowing jacket that paired with it was three quarter length and long sleeved. The color held the tiniest hint of lilac, which seemed to peep through only in a certain light.

Neither of the women wore a veil or a headdress of any kind, but their hair gleamed like silk in the chic, intricate up-do styles they chose. Their natural beauty was enhanced by subtle make-up, but their true beauty was in the happiness and excitement that shone from their eyes.

"Turn around and show us," Grace suggested in her excitement. "We want to see it all."

"You first," Chelsea said to Carrie, deferring to the older sister and stepping back from the landing allowing Carrie to do a full turn without impairment. Carrie gracefully turned half-way around, stopping to allow everyone to see the slim back of her dress, then finished the turn to the front.

After an overstated curtsey and giggles from the gals at the base of the stairs, she did her best Vanna White imitation, stepping backward with arms outstretched toward Chelsea. "Your turn, dear sister." Not to be outdone, Chelsea hammed up the display of her dress as though modeling on a designer's runway in New York City, making two full turns to the applause of her audience. Both were as giddy as young brides could be!

Grace fluttered her eyelids, trying to avoid her tears of joy ruining the makeup she so carefully applied earlier. Maggie put her hands over her mouth in amazement, while Courtney,

Simone and Cassie were grinning like fools. Courtney and Cassie high fived each other, congratulating themselves on the job they had done helping their sisters prepare for this moment. The women all hugged and exclaimed over how wonderful the brides looked as the two joined hands again and gracefully reached the bottom of the stairs.

Courtney ushered them all over to the fireplace in the family room. She designated herself unofficial photographer for the pre-wedding album she was going to create. She had taken various photographs throughout the morning, all un-posed and natural. Now, she would capture some posed shots, then hopefully a few more candid shots later, once this moment was over.

"The guys are going to be speechless when they see you, you both look absolutely stunning," she told them as she snapped pictures of the wedding party women with her new digital camera. *I'm so glad I splurged on this new camera. After all, the brides are getting lots of gifts, so it should be okay that I got one, too. They'll love the great photos this camera takes.* "I've never seen you look more beautiful."

Before they knew it, it was time for the brides to leave. The wedding ceremony was to take place at 10 a.m. so the brides and grooms were to be at the temple by 9. Grace and Maddie would accompany them to help them into their wedding gowns in the brides' room with wall-to-wall mirrors before the ceremony. Everyone hugged as they made their way out the door, heading for the waiting cars. Courtney sniffed back tears as she waved them off, standing with Cassie and Simone in the driveway.

"Come on gals, we've got about half an hour for any last minute primping before we need to leave, too. Courtney, you've smudged your eye make-up by crying, let me fix it for you," Cassie declared, rallying the troops into action.

A few moments later, they were all ready to leave and clambered into the waiting car for the 25-minute ride through the Provo Canyon and north to the temple. The rest of the guests were required to be there by 9.30 a.m. and gather downstairs in the guest area, giving them time to meet and greet and exclaim over how long it had been since they'd seen everyone. With such a large attendance, it was likely to be somewhat chaotic, though quiet lest they be reminded by the temple workers that the temple is a place for quiet reverence. But it's hard to keep the Carpenter clan quiet no matter when and where they get together.

Even though the girls were early, the crowd was already gathering outside where everyone was dressed in his or her Sunday best and chattering animatedly. Hugs were given and accepted in abundance while photographs were being taken everywhere you looked.

The temple looked absolutely stunning, glistening in the morning sun. It was set near the beautiful Mt. Timpanogos to the east, the mountain widely recognized as the sleeping lady to locals. The magnificent white building with its towering spire and arched windows not only featured beautiful grounds, but the stunning backdrop of the majestic mountains behind it made for a photographer's dream location.

It was all so perfect and wonderful, and Courtney managed to hold on to her buoyant mood of earlier. It lasted until the guests began making their way inside. Courtney was left outside, forlorn but trying to be pragmatic and hold on to everything that she learned about the rules governing the use of the temple.

She certainly had plenty of company. All who couldn't attend the ceremony, many nonmembers and those under eighteen were gathered with her, but as she watched the last members of her family disappear into the temple, she realized she had never felt so alone.

As the only member of the immediate Carpenter family left outside, she was the one responsible for representing them among the waiting guests outside. As she mingled, her attention was drawn to the appearance of a large, expensive car pulling up directly in front of the temple to drop off the occupants.

As the occupants got out of the car and signaled the driver to drive on to park the car, she was stunned to see the three members of the Spanish Royal family. She recognized them instantly from the televised announcement they made on the day that Antonio stepped down from his claim to the throne and began to make her way toward them.

"Hello," King Benito called as he spotted her. "I think we may be too late, or too early, depending on how you look at it. I hope that's okay."

"Of course … umm… sir, your majesty, it's a pleasure to meet you," Courtney stammered, not really sure how to address them.

They came to the house when they initially arrived in Utah, but Courtney had been out at the time, spending yet another evening with Peter, quizzing him on the intricacies of his religion. She completely missed their visit with the family, and was now lost as to how to act. She blushed as she realized she had half-curtsied when she spoke.

The King marched up to her, a stern expression on his face. He looked her up and down in an exaggerated manner, taking in her mode of dress and the jewelry she wore. "Are you part of the wedding party?"

"Yes sir, I'm Courtney, Carrie's youngest sister." She held out her hand for him to shake, while the Queen and Princess Adelina looked on in amusement. Adelina stifled a giggle and her mother looked at her sharply with a reproving look Adelina knew all too well.

King Benito shook her hand firmly, looking as if he took the introduction very seriously. "It's an honor to meet yet another member of this delightful Carpenter family."

"It's an honor to meet you too, Your Majesty."

Finally, the king could keep up the pretense no longer, and he burst into booming laughter. "Now, now, while we are here, we are simply tourists, and we are almost family now, are we not? Let's have none of this ceremonial nonsense. I'm Benito, and this is my wife, Isabella and my youngest daughter, Adelina."

Courtney hardly had time to realize he was joking before Adelina flew to her and gripped her in a tight hug. "I'm so pleased to have so many new sisters. I can tell already we're going to be best friends." Adelina broke the hug and kissed Courtney enthusiastically on both cheeks, leaving her open-mouthed.

"Adelina, please! You're startling our hostess, she is not used to the Spanish customs, remember? I'm sorry my dear," Benito took her hand, "my youngest daughter has always been too liberal with her show of affection. She was the same way when she met Carrie at the palace." Isabella stepped forward to extract her daughter and shake Courtney's hand. "Pleasure to meet you, Courtney. That's a beautiful dress you're wearing."

Courtney looked at the finery worn by the family, feeling her own outfit paled in comparison to the glittering display that adorned the Spaniards. "Thank you, and the pleasure's all mine."

Her mind was in a turmoil, she wasn't quite sure what to make of their late appearance, or how to entertain them until the ceremony was over, the very thought of them being royalty was absolutely mind-blowing. She wasn't prepared for this, so thinking on her feet, she tried to imagine how Grace would handle this situation. Her adoptive mother was the perfect host, and if ever Courtney would have wanted her by her side, it was now. She was saved from having to make the next move by the King.

"Well," Benito boomed, clapping his hands together. "What time are we expecting the happy couples to appear?"

Courtney glanced at her watch, almost wilting with relief to see it was nearly 10 a.m. already. "They should be out within the next fifteen minutes or so."

Isabella looked thoughtfully at Courtney. "I have to assume that you are not a Mormon, which is presumably why you are here and not inside this temple? Tell me, my dear, how does it make you feel not being able to attend, are you not upset?"

Courtney chewed her bottom lip, thinking over how honest to be in her answer. Looking around at the enquiring faces, she decided to be completely open. "At first, I wasn't just upset, I was absolutely furious!" she informed them, raising another of the booming laughs from Benito.

"You don't look furious now; will you tell us what changed, Sister, to help us understand it too?" Adelina asked, with genuine interest and concern for her mother. We had a hard time getting Mama to come to the temple at all, which is why we were late. She felt being left standing outside a building was most impolite, to say the least, as well as very unseemly, 'loitering around like hooligans' as she put it. She is also still a little upset by the fact that the next time she sees her son, he will be married in the eyes of the law and God, and she did not witness it,"

Isabella shrugged. "It's true, I do feel that way, I can't help it."

"I can understand why. I have to admit that my understanding and acceptance of the situation was mostly due to a dear friend of mine," Courtney answered with a wry smile. "I think you know him, Peter Anderson?"

Benito nodded. "Yes, we know him, and Antonio explained the happy coincidence that he is a family friend of the Carpenters. Antonio has spoken to us frequently on this matter, but we cannot help but feel excluded, shunned by this new church of his."

Courtney felt the need to try to explain to the Dominguez family as best she could, and to her surprise, she found herself not just repeating Peter's words verbatim, but also genuinely explaining the beliefs, expanding on what he told her with thoughts and feelings of her own that she had no idea she actually held. She would go so far as to say she defended the church and its seemingly unfair rules when relating the events to Peter.

A good-natured debate ensued, with the royal family asking intelligent and well-rounded questions with no animosity, only a desire to learn. Courtney found herself able to answer all their questions, shocked at how much she had absorbed from Peter during their own debates. She was almost disappointed to have the discussion come to an end as the temple doors opened and the guests began piling out, many of them teary-eyed, all happy and very excited.

"Here we go, the couples will come out soon," Courtney explained to her royal guests as the team of official photographers hurried to get in place to catch the best shots of each couple. The small, local companies they approached all balked at the size of the double wedding and in the end two of them agreed to join forces as a team in order to cover the amount of candid and posed pictures that would be required.

"Let's go closer toward the doors. We're immediate family, so no one will mind if we push in toward the front."

True to her word, everyone parted to allow Courtney and the Royal Family to make their way to the front of the gathered guests, allowing them the perfect view of the breathtaking moment when the two couples appeared in the massive doorway of the temple.

A collective sigh of approval, then squeals came from all those who had yet to see the brides in their wedding dresses, Courtney included. The two sisters obviously collaborated on their dresses, being very similar with only slight variances. They both wore the purest white, mermaid silhouette dresses that showed off their tall, slender frames to perfection without being overly figure hugging. The material for both was of the finest satin, overlaid with the same beautiful and intricate applique and embroidery.

The same pattern adorned the lace sleeves, full length for Carrie and three-quarter for Chelsea. Carrie's neckline was high collared with a slight 'v', ending at the top of her breastbone, showing off the small, subtle diamond pendant Antonio had presented her with as his wedding day gift. Chelsea's neckline was square, the shoulders sitting so as to give the merest hint of her creamy skin and showing off her long, swanlike neck.

Both had only the smallest touch of a train, the lace covering the satin pooling ever so slightly on the floor around their feet. A row of tiny satin-covered buttons adorned the dresses at the back, running from the collar down to the tops of the thighs. Their matching satin slippers peeped from below the dresses as they stood smiling at the crowd and the photographers, their men handsome and proud beside them.

The grooms were stunning in their matching black tuxedos with black cumber buns, smiling from ear to ear, obviously each one very proud of the bride on his arm.

They planned that Carrie and Antonio would exit first for the traditional couple photos as they stepped through the doors, allowing their assigned photographers to capture the moment. As they stepped aside into the crowd Chelsea and Kade took their turn to be photographed exiting the temple doors before joining the excited group, only to be posed here and there at the whim of their photographers.

The girls still looked radiantly beautiful and demure, and for the first time, Courtney truly understood the special meaning of carrying out this day in a pure form, and giving yourself in your entirety to just one person, for the rest of your existence in life and in the eternities.

Once again, her thoughts surprised her and she longed to talk with Peter about them. There was no time for that now as the gathering was being herded into groups by the photographers and it was time to take their places. Now Courtney would be fully included in the proceedings and take her place by her sisters as part of the wedding party.

Before she could make her way to her sisters, she felt someone grab her around the waist and twirl her around. Peter took her hand and led her to their assigned positions with the wedding party. He was, after all, a best man.

Chapter Six

"Are you all alright for refreshments?" Courtney stood by the Dominguez family, noting their lack of glasses in front of them and wondering why the serving staff hadn't been more attentive.

"We grew a little tired of punch, some coffee would be wonderful, my dear," Benito replied.

Isabella sucked in a sharp breath. "Benito!" she scolded.

"Oh, of course, please forgive me. I am still getting used to the finer points of my son's new religion. I forgot coffee is not an option."

Courtney grinned, feeling at ease with the family now after spending so much time in their company. "Oh, coffee is most definitely an option! I'm not a Mormon either, and therefore, I have my own supply in the house. It's a good quality roast and I'm sure it'll be to your taste. How do you like it?"

"Ahhhh … a girl after my own heart! (Did I say that right?)," Benito said with a smile. "Small, strong and black is the Spanish way, but we are willing to experiment, since we are here as tourists to learn the American ways."

"No problem, I'll inform the caterers. Would you all like a cup?"

All three heads nodded and Courtney dashed off to instruct one of the catering staff on preparing coffee for four, then hurried back to her guests as fast as her full-length, deep blue gown would allow her.

"Coffee will be here shortly," she announced breezily as she returned to the table, once again the usual Courtney who took everything in stride after her earlier stumbling at the temple.

"Great, is it American style coffee?" Adelina asked enthusiastically. "We went to a coffee house the other day and I had this huge coffee that was all creamy and filled with caramel. It was so delicious."

"It looked absolutely revolting," Benito replied, screwing up his face.

An enthusiastic debate over coffee styles ensued and by the time the server appeared with the tray, the group was engaged in an animated discussion. When Antonio appeared and began speaking with his family, Courtney was able to excuse herself and take her leave, saying she needed to mingle. She roamed around through the reception party guests, chatting, laughing and ensuring everyone had everything they needed. She didn't want anyone else to be worrying about the guests tonight.

Once satisfied that everyone was having a great time and she hadn't missed speaking to anyone, she decided it was time for a breather. The party was in full swing, the brides and grooms were deeply in love and having a great time, and she was feeling happy and relaxed.

The rest of the day went wonderfully; the ring ceremony was held under an intricate arch of fragrant blooms immediately after everyone arrived at the Carpenter estate. The brides and their bridesmaids carried stunning bouquets. The parents were all seated in the front rows, followed by the other guests who filled the remaining chairs while some stood as the beaming brides and grooms walked down the aisle arm-in-arm toward their Bishop.

It had been exciting to watch the couples exchange rings while their bridesmaids and best men stood proudly by their sides. The simple service provided a beautiful, touching ceremony for those who could not attend the temple earlier.

Courtney no longer felt left out of the proceedings. She hoped the Dominguez family felt the same now as they, too, had been included in all the events.

The intimate lunch for the family and close friends had also been joyful, with lots of hearty banter and the showing of a slideshow of photographs of the couples in various stages of their lives, together and apart. There had been much one-upmanship and many a red face with the story telling and joking.

A great time had been enjoyed by all. Following the lunch, everyone returned to their homes to change, relax and take naps, and gather their energy for the evening reception.

Now, as twilight gave way to darkness, the richness of the setting and the amazing decorations came into view. A million twinkle lights illuminated the grounds, creating a magical clearing in an enchanted wood. Everyone was having a good time. *Despite the no alcohol policy, Mormons sure know how to party,* Courtney thought.

The large dance floor was filled to capacity, the spread was enormous and people wandered around with plates, exclaiming over the delights the platters provided. Even those who attended the family luncheon only a few short hours before were ravenous to try all the delights of the evening. Several flavors of punches adorned the serving tables, the crystal sparkling in the twinkle lights. The servers moved expertly through the crowds with their trays of colorful drinks, ensuring no one went without for long.

Courtney was choked up by the first dance; both couples looked so graceful and so in love as they whirled around the dance floor. The father-daughter dance was also a moving experience. Since John Carpenter was only there in spirit, Carrie danced with her brother Carter while Chelsea danced with Nigel, Maggie's husband. He was as much a part of the family as Maggie and Simone were, and it seemed only fitting that the main male influence in their lives since the death of their father would have this honor. Half-way through the dance, the girls exchanged partners, much to the delight of the watching crowd. It had all been so beautiful and heartwarming.

With the sit-down meal over, the formal seating plan in the marquee was abandoned, with tables all moved to outside surrounding the specially constructed dance floor and stage. The dance floor in the marquee had served its purpose for the official dances, but it was much too pleasant an evening to stay cooped up in there. The revelers had gladly moved to the tables set up around the outside of the floor where the walls of the marquee had been rolled up, ensuring a gentle breeze flowing through. Tables were moved around at will so friends could sit with friends to enjoy the music and dancing.

Courtney took this moment to duck out and observe from a short distance away, leaning against an ancient and dignified old oak at the rear of the merriment. She smiled as she watched Chelsea and Kade on the dance floor, her upper body pulled tightly against him, her cheek pressed against his chest as they swayed to the slow love song the band was playing. For the moment, any fears her sister might have had for what was to come that night were far from her mind.

Instinctively, Courtney scanned the crowd for Peter. Her heart skipped a beat as she located him. He was standing beside a lone Antonio, who was looking forlornly at his bride as she was commandeered on the dance floor once more. She watched Peter slap Antonio's back and say something that made Antonio rock with laughter, brightening his brooding features. Peter was such a good man, so keen to make everyone around him happy.

Reluctantly, she dragged her eyes away from Peter, looking to see how Antonio's family was faring in the gathering since she'd left them. She soon saw there was no need to worry about them. Benito was holding court with a group of men, the talk appearing animated and amusing. Isabella was talking to a group of women, her eyes frequently darting to her son and smiling with deep affection and contentment. Adelina was simply charming everyone with her beyond-her-years wisdom and her childlike delight of everything American. Everybody was just fine.

Peaceful satisfaction soon turned to distress. There was only one blot on this beautiful landscape for Courtney that night. She watched now as a man made his way over to the closest bar area and waited impatiently while yet another glass of punch was filled for him. As he turned to walk away, Courtney noticed the slight sway and the uneven gait as he made his way back to a table he'd pulled back away from the crowds.

She watched as he took a large gulp of the punch, grimaced, and pulled a flask from his inside jacket pocket. He slowly unscrewed the small lid and tipped a generous measure of the liquid into his glass. Courtney's eyes narrowed. The flask she had seen him producing earlier had a leather trim, this one didn't.

David Fisher, otherwise known as her 'natural father,' was onto at least his second flask of the night. Courtney shook her head as he took a sip and smugly leaned back in his chair, stretching his long legs out in front of him and crossing them at the ankles. She knew the liquid inside the flask would be whisky, either premium or cheap gut rot depending on the state of his finances at the moment.

Even his appearance made him stand out a mile from the other guests. His black hair was now heavily streaked with premature grey and the several-day-old stubble on his face was completely grey. He had gone to the effort of wearing a jacket and shirt, but the grey material of both was unmatched and creased, its drabness accentuated by the beautiful setting and riots of color surrounding him.

The shirt was open by several buttons and he hadn't bothered with a tie, not even for the ring ceremony. Accompanying the shirt and jacket were stiff pants of black denim, a belt sporting a large, garish, silver buckle depicting an etched rodeo horse mid-buck, the rider hanging on with one hand and raising his cowboy hat high in the air with the other. The outfit was completed with battered and worn tan cowboy boots; from her viewpoint, Courtney could make out the holes in the raised soles.

Idly, she wondered why he bothered coming. She begged Grace not to invite him, pleaded that he would only cause trouble. Her request fell on deaf ears. Grace was far too polite not to invite her sister's widower to a family wedding, even though he was rarely included in other events.

Courtney figured she'd better keep an eye on this man and try to determine just how drunk he was. Like many alcoholics, his tolerance for booze was phenomenal, being able to put away quantities that would have most people unconscious on the floor. She guessed the body built up a tolerance and it took more and more to hit that high and reach the required buzz. Or, in her father's case, numbness.

At the moment, it didn't look like he was about to cause a scene, or that he had any intention of interacting with the family or guests at all. He likely accepted the invitation just to partake of the great food since he knew the drinks wouldn't suit his taste.

Her summation of his current situation could change in a single mouthful more; she had seen it many times.

As she kept a careful watch, her mind drifted back to her early years. Her mother loved to tell her the story of how she fell in love with the rugged Texan at first sight. He was so different from the wholesome, clean-cut young men she knew from church.

She had been intrigued and excited by him, so much so that she shunned everything to be with him, leaving behind her family and the church to set up house with him. It hadn't been long before Courtney came along, but as far as she was concerned, it had never really been a happy family.

Looking back on her baby pictures of her with her father, there always seemed to be a beer bottle in some corner of every photo. Her toddler memories were of desperately trying to please him by going along with the activities he wanted. She mentally flicked through the photo album in her head. There she was sitting on the hood of his oversized truck, or she was on his fishing boat, having endured a predawn start to spend the day with him, struggling to hold up his catch while the line cut into her pudgy hands.

She'd spent her childhood trying to impress him and elicit a kind word or some praise, to live up to his desire for her to "act like a Texan." Not only could she ride, but she could ride like a rodeo stuntwoman. He tried to teach her to shoot, but at five years old when he first placed the gun in her hands and told her to aim for the line of empty bottles, the deafening blast and force of the recoil terrified her.

She dropped the gun and ran screaming for her mother. It was a full hour before the ringing in her ears stopped enough to hear his taunts and jeers. No matter how angry he got, she refused to go near a gun ever again; the mere sight of it would make her cry.

Her mother did her best to stand up to him, but she was no match for his six-foot-three-inch frame and overbearing manner. While he was tender and loving with his wife, Lucy, he was completely different with his daughter.

As she grew older, Courtney came to the conclusion that he was disappointed in her, that he wanted a son, and this daughter was a poor substitute. It was the only thing she could think of to explain his attitude toward her. In a desperate attempt to make him proud, she tried to give him what he wanted, sacrificing any femininity in the hope of gaining his approval. It didn't work.

He had always been a drinker, but when her mother, Lucy, was diagnosed with cancer, his habit spiraled out of control. By the time she passed, his breakfast consisted of beer and V-8® juice mixed. He drank mostly beer throughout the day without eating much food and then consumed a full bottle of whisky every night. She supposed she would have coped if Grace hadn't rescued her from that environment.

During her mother's illness, she already learned to cook, clean, and look after herself, tiptoeing around the man who spent his days and nights sitting in the darkened den in an armchair, staring into space, only moving to lift the glass to his lips.

Still, she was so relieved when Grace took her away from the situation. It was only meant to be temporary, just until her father pulled himself together and got over his grief. That had been over sixteen years ago, and there was no improvement. One thing she could say for certain, David Fisher may have loved his wife, but he did not care a plug nickel about his daughter.

Grace took her to visit David once a week in her youth, but he barely acknowledged their presence and certainly didn't seem pleased to see her. Courtney didn't know much about the events that occurred leading up to the adoption, but it didn't seem as if he fought for her at all. She kept up the visits until she was sixteen, when her teenage rebellion roared against the injustice and she cast him from her life as much as the family would allow. He made no effort to contact her.

When she was nineteen, a sense of duty and concern made her want to check up on him, but the visits were mostly silent and awkward, her father permanently drunk. Courtney admitted she was uncomfortable in his company, but she persevered on a once-a-week basis, even though she dreaded it.

Remembering those times was too difficult. She shook her head, trying to clear it of the unhappy memories from those childhood years. Her life was spectacular now and she had an amazing family including a terrific adoptive father, John, when he was alive.

Now she just wished this man wasn't here, ruining the reception for her. As she watched him, he gave up the pretense of the punch, tipping back his head and raising the flask, emptying the contents in huge gulps, shaking it to ensure he released every last drop. He returned the flask to his pocket, retrieved the other one, and repeated the action, slamming it down in anger as he realized that it, too, was empty.

"What kind of wedding doesn't serve booze?"

Courtney could hear his annoyed ramblings clearly from her vantage point.

"Not even damn champagne for the damn toasts, what a freakin' joke. Bunch of pious, self-righteous, self-serving assholes."

The last word was accompanied by hands smashing down onto the table, and as her father rose to his feet, Courtney sprinted into action. It was time to try to get him out of here, and preferably with as little commotion as possible.

"Dad! Hey Dad," she called as she tried to hurry toward him, hampered by her gown and heels. The tall man stopped and turned at the sound of her voice. Courtney always wondered where she had gotten her short gene from, David Fisher was 6 feet 3 inches tall, and her mother had been almost six feet.

The Carpenters were all tall too, and Courtney had spent most of her life feeling like a midget. As a result, she learned early the power of a precariously high, spiked heel. In spite of all the practice she'd had, the set of tables at the rear were placed on grass, and she tried to tiptoe while holding her dress up out the way.

"Well, well, if it ain't Cinderella herself," her father drawled as he watched her ridiculous, hurried approach.

Courtney tried to plaster a pleasant and friendly smile on her face as she reached him. "Hi there, I was just coming to talk to you, where are you off to?"

"Going to see if any of those fine fellows down there can spare a man a shot."

With the slur of his words and the slight sway as he stood there, Courtney realized he was far more drunk than she had initially imagined. This left her in a quandary. He arrived in his own car and as much as she wanted him out of there, her conscience would not allow her to let him drive.

She tried not to let her dismay show on her face. Instead, she responded to his statement. "Come on, you know as well as I do that they won't have any booze, they're all Mormons. How about you and I go inside and have some coffee, I've got a secret stash."

Her father closed one eye to focus on her, obviously seeing two of her when both were open. "Oh well, that's the height of badness isn't it." He snorted. "Secret stash, coffee for crap's sake. You're as much a goody-two-shoes as the rest of them. But see, I know better."

He tapped his nose with his finger as he swayed in front of Courtney. "They ain't half what they pretend to be, bunch of hypocrites. You can't tell me that none of those fine gentleman down there …" He raised his arm to indicate the happy crowd packed around the dance floor, almost knocking himself off balance. "… don't have a little snifter tucked away that they toot on when they think nobody's looking."

Courtney tried to laugh off his sarcasm and slur against the party guests. "I'm pretty sure I *can* tell you that, Dad." She placed a cajoling hand on his arm. "Look, you need to come inside with me and have some coffee."

Her father bent down to leer into her face and she recoiled from the stench of alcohol on his breath. He threw her arm off his and practically growled at her. "And who might you be to go telling me what I need to do, what gives you the right?"

"The fact that I care what happens here tonight, and care what happens to you is what gives me the right. For heaven's sake, I'm not your enemy, I'm your daughter." Courtney was losing patience now and her words were sharp.

"Well, now, that's what you think, what most people think, but some of us know different, even some of your perfect family. Oh, they ain't nearly as saintly as they pretend to be. You ask Lady Grace why you're the family's dirty little secret, then you'll know you've got no claim on me. Now, push off."

David managed to focus his vision enough to give her a hearty push to the chest, causing her to take several steps back to maintain her balance on those heels. Suddenly, Peter and Antonio were by her side, holding her to steady her balance.

"Everything alright here, Courtney?"

Peter's voice was gentle and Courtney forced herself to forget about the words she had just heard, and deal with the here and now situation. "Not really, my father," ... it was her turn now to let the words drip with sarcasm ... "is about to leave, but

I'm afraid he's had a lot to drink and can't drive. I'm trying to figure out a way to get him home, leaving the back way."

The two men picked up her tone and meaning instantly. David turned to the newcomers, squaring up to face them. Although Courtney knew that nothing could be farther from the truth, Antonio had such dark features and brooding expression, he actually looked stern, if not downright menacing, at the best of times. Right now, he was angry, and that dark, Spanish passion was barely concealed, his eyes flashing fire, every muscle in his body tensed, ready to explode. Peter was immediately talking, trying to diffuse the tension.

"Why don't I drive him home in his car, Antonio can follow in one of your cars, Courtney, then we can come back together."

"You're the groom and the best man, you can't just disappear from the wedding and it wouldn't be fair, this is your special night." She didn't voice her thoughts that she didn't want Peter to be alone with her father either. Peter was all man, but he was gentle and kind. He probably didn't have a violent bone in his body and alone, he would be no match for David Fisher if he decided he didn't like the way things were turning out.

The impossible situation was eased slightly as Benito, alerted to the situation by Isabella who had been unable to take her eyes off her son practically the whole night, marched up to the small group. Peter's father, James Anderson, was hot on his heels.

"Is there some sort of problem here?" Benito boomed in his imposing voice. Courtney cringed, hoping it hadn't carried over the music provided by the band. If they attracted any more attention, the entire wedding party would be up here in a moment and she would just die of shame on the spot.

"Not a problem as such, Father. This gentleman finds himself with the need of an escort home, and Peter and I have offered our services. My new sister feels it would not be proper for me to leave my own wedding, that's all."

Benito was a politician and a leader. Courtney watched as he listened to his son's words, hearing more of what he didn't say than what he did, and then glanced around the small gathering, measuring the situation. "I agree it would not be proper. Do not worry, the solution is simple. James and I will escort this man home. Does he have a vehicle here?"

"Yes, round the back," Courtney informed him.

"Don't talk about me as if I'm not here, and who the hell says I wanna go home?"

Benito turned to David, the other men instinctively moving to his side. Courtney almost giggled. The four impeccably dressed men facing down her drunken lout of a father was quite a sight. She didn't have her camera, but the picture would forever be emblazoned in her mind.

Benito was the first to break the staring contest. "You, sir, are drunk, and in the home of gracious hosts who abhor alcohol and do not permit it on their premises. You have forfeited all right to be treated with any respect or consideration, or even as a decent human being, which you obviously are not. You will follow our instructions without complaint, or there will be consequences."

David dropped his gaze and relaxed his stance, backing down under proffered force of the four. If the situation hadn't been so dire, Courtney felt she might have been able to enjoy that moment. Benito, with his thick accent and precise English sounded like something out of a movie. She let her imagination run wild as she wondered what those consequences he spoke of might be. While she did, Benito was issuing orders all round.

"James, you and I will take this man's car and give him a ride home in it. Peter, you follow us in my rental car and you can drive us back. Antonio, get back to the wedding party and see to your bride. Assure your mother that all is well. Courtney, do not worry, we have *everything* under control."

With the emphasis on the word 'everything,' and his subtle wink to her, she knew that Benito fully understood the situation and the nature of the man he was dealing with. He would be prepared and take precautions. She was left standing with Antonio as the other three marched David Fisher along to the drive to the rear of the house, two flanked on the sides of the man, the third bringing up the rear.

She turned to Antonio. "Thanks for all your help, I really appreciate it."

"You're welcome."

"I don't know how you noticed something was wrong so quickly, but I'm glad you turned up when you did."

Antonio chuckled softly. "I cannot take credit for it, you have your date to thank for that."

Courtney looked at him in confusion. "I don't have a date tonight."

"You don't think so? Then tell me why Peter has barely been able to focus on the matters at hand since we arrived back here? He was the perfect best man at the temple ceremony, but since then, well let's just say that his attention has been held elsewhere."

Antonio was grinning at her, his smile lighting up his face and banishing that brooding look. "Peter? You think Peter is my date?"

"If he isn't, he wants to be. He hasn't taken his eyes off you the whole night."

Courtney raised a hand to carry out her nervous habit before remembering the effort that had gone into attempting to smooth down her usual soft spikes into something chic and sophisticated. She dropped her hand helplessly and shrugged at Antonio, not knowing what to say. Still laughing, he decided to have mercy on her.

"I can see my words have thrown you somewhat; I will go and leave you to consider them."

Antonio gave her a short bow and straightened to leave. "Oh, thank you again, and I'm sorry about my father," Courtney called as he began to walk away.

Antonio turned back, looking at her sadly, his face now etched with concern. "You have nothing to apologize for, and from what I overheard, no claim to that odious man. The words may have come as a shock, but I think that taking everything into consideration, it would be a very good thing if it turned out to be the truth."

Courtney went beet red. "Oh, umm, you heard that huh?"

"I'm sorry, we couldn't help it."

"No problem, thanks again. Now get back to Carrie before she accuses me of stealing her husband."

Courtney tried to make light of the situation, backing away from Antonio before finally turning and attempting to sprint to the house. Giving up the attempt, she paused, kicked off her shoes, and left them lying on the grass as she ran barefoot for the sanctuary of her home.

Once there, she charged up the stairs, entered her bedroom and flung herself on her bed. For all the events that had transpired, there was one thought running through her head.

Peter heard David Fisher say I am nothing but a dirty little secret. This night was probably one of the worst of her life, and there were quite a few contenders for that honor. She buried her face into her mountain of pillows and began to cry.

Chapter Seven

Courtney woke the next morning with her eyes feeling puffy and gritty. She had no idea at what point the crying was overtaken by sleep, but she didn't feel she'd enjoyed a restful night. By the color of the light trying to peep its way through the curtains and the silence from outside, she guessed that dawn had not long broken.

She rose stiffly, still in her party gown from the night before and made her way to the window. Sure enough, the sky was still burning with an orangey glow, the birds were loudly greeting another morning, and the equipment and decorations from yesterday's celebration were all still in place. She knew that in an hour or two, the garden would be a hive of activity as people arrived to disassemble everything and pack it into their waiting trucks.

She walked over to her door and listened carefully. The house appeared to be still and silent. She desperately wanted to go downstairs, make a pot of coffee and take a mug out to the stables. She loved sitting in the hay talking to the horses; they made the best listeners and nothing cheered her up quite like their gentle wickers and soft nudges from their velvet muzzles.

There was no way Mom would let Maggie, Nigel and Simone work the day after a party, though the kitchen was probably buzzing with temporary staff who would handle the clean-up and have the run of the house for the day. She really didn't want to see a single soul right now, but could she sweep into the kitchen, prepare her coffee and slip out without chatting to them, like some snobby lady of the manor from an English period drama? *No, I couldn't,* she admitted with a sigh. *I could never be that rude. Not even today.*

She wandered into her bathroom and washed her face, not even daring to first look at her reflection that would show her streaked makeup, hair probably half gelled down and the other half sticking out in all directions, bloodshot eyes, and a sourpuss face. Once she scrubbed away what she physically could from the night before, she carefully brushed the styling product from her hair, allowing it to return to its soft, shaped spikes.

She returned to her bedroom feeling a little more human. She shimmied her way out of the gown and changed her clothes quickly, desperate to get out before anyone else woke up. She opted for a t-shirt, jeans and sneakers. As she was tying her laces, she heard movement from the hallway. *Crap, someone else is up.*

It dawned on her that it could only be Grace; her sisters had booked bridal suites in two hotels in Salt Lake City for their wedding night. Today, they would be off on their respective honeymoons. That thought turned her attention to the weddings of the night before. She had run out on them, had missed the cutting of the cakes, the toss of two wedding bouquets. *What a disappointment I must be to this family all the way around. I didn't even stay to see my sisters off on their honeymoons!*

Her mood brightened just a bit as she allowed herself a small giggle when she wondered if Cassie and Kade had figured everything out. By the looks of things on the dance floor, they would have been just fine. She had no need to worry about Carrie. Antonio not only oozed sex appeal, but he radiated prowess. With such a self-assured and probably experienced partner, she figured Carrie would be in a daze the entire honeymoon. She had to admit, her sisters found two exceedingly hot guys, but they couldn't hold a candle to Peter in her eyes. The smile fell from her face as she remembered Peter and the words he overheard last night.

Unable to face Grace until she had time to think, Courtney did something she hadn't done since she was eighteen. Opening her large sash window, she slipped through the opening and carefully reached for the branches of the mature oak that grew outside her window. Once she had a firm hold of the close branches, she swung herself over and sure-footedly found her way down through the tree as if it had been yesterday, her muscle memory carrying out the moves with easy familiarity. She dropped the last few feet to the ground below, landing with a soft thud. Not waiting to see if the sound had attracted attention, she sprinted round the side of the house and made her way to the stables.

Reaching Ice's stable, she greeted her old friend. As Courtney stood with her cheek pressed against the gentle animal's graceful neck, stroking her gently, she recalled the moment she had first seen her. A few days after her arrival at the

Carpenter home when she had spent most of her time hiding in her new room, over-awed by her surroundings and deep in grief for the loss of her mother, Chelsea had been sent to summon her. Her sister's eyes had been filled with excitement as she tried to keep her face serious when she told Courtney her Daddy had requested her presence out in the yard.

Wondering what she had done wrong and what her punishment was to be, Courtney followed Chelsea silently, thinking that her cousin seemed delighted to see her in trouble. Reaching the yard, she found both Grace and John standing at a stable door. She dragged her feet as she approached, waiting for them to start yelling at her. John's face was serious as he spoke.

"Courtney, you have a home here for as long as you want it, you're family now. You always have been, although we haven't seen much of you up until now. There is something that we know you love doing, and here we have facilities for you to do it whenever you want. Of course, it comes with a lot of responsibility and a lot of hard work. Are you willing to take on that hard work and responsibility along with the fun of it too?"

Courtney swallowed. *So this was it, I'm the poor relative and I'm going to have to work for my keep. I'll be allowed to ride the horses but I have to do all the mucking out and grooming and take care of the tack.* She decided it was a fair trade; she was no stranger to hard work and she did love horses. Her father had been determined she should ride like a rodeo star from an early age, so he had her in the saddle over at the breeding ranch where he worked. She knew how to care for horses. She nodded at John, accepting the terms.

He stepped forward and opened the stable door, and out gamboled the most beautiful creature Courtney had ever seen. She was tall and gangly still, but her features were already displaying the dished face, arched neck and high tail carriage that marked her as an Arabian. She was also the purest white Courtney had ever seen on a horse, and in the sunshine, she looked like freshly fallen snow on a mid-winter late morning.

"Oh, she's so beautiful," Courtney had gasped and the words were echoed from behind her, along with gasps of delight. Courtney turned to see the other children gathered in a group watching, a few feet back from her.

"This little filly is only two years old, so she can't be ridden yet. I saw her a few days ago on my business trip. For the entertainment, they arranged a day out at a horse sale, of all things." John grimaced as he recalled the scene. "This little one didn't even seem to be halter broken; she was panicking and bucking around like crazy. She was far too young to be there, and I knew I just had to get her out. She's been staying with a friend of mine since then, giving her a chance to calm down before the long trip. Besides, the very moment I saw her, I thought of you, Courtney. I was hoping we could raise her together, undo the damage and halter break her properly, what do you think?"

Courtney's head was already racing with ideas on how to gently train the horse and get her used to tack. She'd soaked up everything at her father's workplace; she was sure she knew just what to do. She smiled as she watched the young filly run around on her long, spindly legs, exploring her surroundings. "I'd love to help you, Uncle John."

This was all new to Courtney; she didn't yet know John as anything but 'Uncle John.' Later, after her formal adoption she would begin to call him 'Dad,' reflecting the genuine love she felt for him.

She saw John and Grace exchange a look and a smile between them. "You wouldn't be helping me; I'd be helping you."

She didn't understand the difference. Instead, she called to the young horse, emulating the sounds she had heard the breeder make to the foals. The filly instantly responded, making her way over to Courtney and butting her with her head, investigating her pockets for treats. Courtney giggled as she stroked her graceful, slender neck. "What's her name?"

"She doesn't have one yet. Since she's your horse, we thought you should name her."

It took a few moments for the words to sink in, then Courtney looked up at John with a confused expression. "What do you mean?"

"I mean just what I said, she belongs to you. She's a gift to you, from all of us. We all have horses, and you're one of us now, so you deserve one of your own too, although you're welcome to ride any one you choose at any time. If you don't like her, we can exchange her or sell her when she's a little older.

If you leave, you can take her with you. If there's something else you'd rather have…."

John allowed his sentence to trail off, a look of worry and anticipation on his face.

"There is nothing else I'd rather have in the whole wide world! I can't believe she's mine. Thank you so much, Uncle John."

Courtney flung herself into his arms, overwhelmed and overjoyed. Her cousins cheered and clapped, and embarrassed by her show of affection, Courtney pulled away and turned all business. "If I'm allowed to name her, I'm going to call her Ice," she declared. She rubbed her fingers together thoughtfully. "Her coat is a little grimy, has she ever been brushed?"

"I don't know, but I doubt it. There are stalls over there, just off the tack room; would you like to see what she makes of it?"

Courtney grinned at John and strode off toward the stalls, the gangly filly trotting after her happily. From that moment on, the two had been the best of friends.

Now, Ice turned and nudged her, whickering softly. Courtney realized that as she had been lost in the memories, tears had been streaming down her cheeks, soaking the mare's coat.

She looked into the gentle eyes, ones so dark they looked like they were lined with eyeliner. "I'm sorry girl; I'm getting you all wet."

She wiped at the snow-white coat with her T-shirt, trying to dry up the tears. "Why do good people have to leave you so soon, eh girl? First Mom, then John. This life just isn't fair, is it? Gosh, I'm a mess today." She wiped at her eyes and cheeks, then spoke again as she stroked Ice's muzzle. "Don't fret, I'll be okay, I just have some things to think about, that's all.

Ice tossed her mane, shaking her head. Courtney laughed. "Well, tough, I'm going to do it anyway."

She curled up in the corner of the loosebox, snuggling down in the hay. Forcing herself, she recalled her father's words from the night before. He hadn't actually said the words outright, but he'd implied heavily that she wasn't his daughter and he wasn't the only one who knew it. He had said she had no claim to him, but that didn't count for much. He had always considered himself akin to a wild mustang, belonging to and answering to no one. Could it really be true, or was it just the ramblings of a drunken fool, words said to hurt at a time when he wanted her to back off and leave him alone?

If he's not my father, then who is he? And who the heck is my real father?

As far as she knew, her mother left her church and her family to run off with David Fisher. It was an instant infatuation leading to a quick wedding. Where was there time for anyone else to be involved? It made no sense. Unless her mother had an affair after she was married, but that didn't seem like something her mother would do. Besides, that wouldn't really make her a 'dirty little secret.'

If her mother's actions were shameful to the family, it would have been when she abandoned the church in the first place. There had never been any animosity between the sisters that she knew of, only her father's strong dislike for the Carpenters. He had even laid down the law that she and her mom were to have little contact with Lucy's family.

Courtney felt she was going round in circles. One thing her father, if she could even think of him that way anymore, had said was that Grace knew the truth and had implied she had covered it up. That had to be a lie! Grace was the most wonderful, honest and upfront person she knew.

Maybe everything was a lie! Maybe this family had never loved her, never wanted her, and she was just some undesirable embarrassment they'd had to put up with to protect the family name or something, having no choice. Since they could no longer sweep her under the rug, they had brought her here and tried to make her respectable instead. Maybe Lucy Rae Carpenter Fisher wasn't even her mother!

That had to be it, but whose little bastard was she then? Her cousins were young then. Could she be the result of a transgression by John or Grace, given away to her sister to raise? All this time, they pretended she was truly a part of this family, fed her, clothed her, given her a happy late childhood, then a job and a wonderful life, all the time pretending they were upstanding, respectable members of the Church. Courtney was furious; it was time to confront Grace and get some answers.

Leaping to her feet, she startled Ice. Taking a few deep breaths, she tried to calm her inner rage so she could soothe the old mare before she left her. She stroked and whispered to her, causing the mare's silky ears to flick back and forth at the sound of her voice.

Certain she was fine now, Courtney eased her way gently out of the stall. Once the door was closed behind her, she jogged back round to the front of the house. By the time she reached the door, her rage was back in full force and before she could rethink her actions, she went in search of Grace.

She found her sitting in the family room, sipping a glass of orange juice and watching the activity in the grounds as the various companies arrived to collect their belongings. Grace turned to smile at her and she stopped dead center in the room.

"There you are, Courtney. I was concerned. Nobody has seen you for a while. Where did you disappear to last night?"

"I'm surprised anyone even noticed I was gone," Courtney replied, allowing her anger to drip from her words.

Grace looked surprised. "Of course we did, especially when it was time to see the couples off."

"Well, I had a *situation* to deal with; I bet none of you even noticed that."

Now Grace looked worried. "What kind of situation? Are you alright?"

"My father," she almost spat the words at Grace, "was drunk as a skunk and hell bent on creating a scene."

"Oh, my goodness! Oh, dear, I'm so sorry Courtney. You did tell me not to invite him; I should have listened."

Grace hung her head, obviously believing this was the sole source of Courtney's dissatisfaction. "You must have handled it well then, because no one mentioned any scene."

"I couldn't have handled it on my own actually. Thankfully, Peter and his father, and Antonio and Benito assisted and escorted him off the premises."

Grace nodded. "I'm glad they were there to help you, although I am terribly ashamed they were involved in it. I suppose I have no one to blame but myself for insisting he be invited. To be honest, I never thought he would come, he hates this family."

"And why exactly is that?"

Grace shrugged. "I don't know for sure, but I guess because I tried to talk Lucy out of marrying him, and he felt that we would always try to influence her to come home, either to us or to the church."

"Did you? Try to influence her I mean."

"Of course I did. Every chance I got. Not about the church, that had to be her decision, but about coming home. Well, at least later on I did. That man is nothing but a drunk. I'm sure he loved her. You can see what losing Lucy has done to him, but he wasn't good for her and he certainly wasn't good for you. How he treated you made Lucy miserable."

"Why?"

Grace looked at her, shocked. "Because she was your mother, because you were the light of her life and she loved you more than anything else in the world, that's why. Courtney, why are you asking all these questions? What exactly happened last night?"

Courtney ignored Grace's questions and instead concentrated on her pale face and shrill tone. It certainly looked like she might have something to hide. "Was she really my mother?"

Grace's already pale face went ashen. This time her answer was almost a whisper. "Yes, she was, and she sacrificed everything for you. Why would you question that?"

Courtney sat heavily on the nearest chair, relief flooding her. She knew that Grace had and was still keeping something from her, but at least her mother truly had been her mother. Grace would never lie directly to her that way.

"Courtney, please, tell me what happened, what's been said?"

Courtney chewed on her bottom lip, some of her anger dissipating and leaving her with a sense of despair. It felt like she no longer knew who she was, that she had lost her entire identity. She decided the only way to resolve this was to stop being angry with Grace and talk with her openly.

"Last night, Dad said that I had no claim on him and hinted strongly that I wasn't his daughter at all. He also said I was just a 'dirty little secret,' one that the Carpenters had been covering up, you in particular."

Grace sighed deeply and dropped her head, suddenly looking closer to her actual age than she had ever done before. She took a moment before she raised her head and looked Courtney in the eye. "This all had to come out one day, I guess. Wait here."

Courtney was left alone with her thoughts as Grace left the room. She felt displaced, almost dreamlike, as if this entire situation was some horrible nightmare from which she would soon awaken. She wanted to cry again, but didn't want to let anybody see her weakness. If she wanted to get all the answers, she had to remain stoic and determined. When Grace returned, Courtney had steeled herself against whatever was to come.

Grace was carrying a wooden box, which she then placed on the coffee table before taking a seat on the coach. "Will you come and sit beside me, so I can show you this?"

Courtney rose and went to sit by Grace, saying nothing. She looked at the box, which appeared to be antique, taking in its highly lacquered wood and its delicate patterns of mother of pearl inlays. It was beautiful, special, but Courtney could only imagine the horrors it might hold within. Taking a tiny, silver key, Grace unlocked the box and opened it, revealing a stack of paperwork stored inside.

Courtney noticed the slight shake of her hands as Grace rummaged through the papers. Locating the one she wanted, she held it out to Courtney. Taking it, Courtney dropped her eyes to peruse it, coming face to face for the first time with her original birth certificate.

Scanning through the document, relief overwhelmed her as she saw the section for mother filled in with the name Lucy Rae Carpenter in an ornate script. Although Grace had reassured her, seeing it in black and white made it actually real. She had no idea of the extent to which Grace had lied to her as yet, and tears pricked her eyes when she confirmed that the mother she adored had really been what she believed her to be … her mother. That part of her life wasn't a lie at least.

Moving on to the section for her father's details, she was surprised to read the name Zachary Edward Ballantyne. She looked at Grace, confusion clear in her eyes. She hadn't known what she expected, but it wasn't a name she had never heard of. "What's this?"

"The name of your real father."

"So it's true then? David Fisher isn't my father, and you have been lying to me all my life."

Grace nodded miserably. "I guess there really isn't any other way to put it."

Courtney had never seen Grace so defeated. She was a strong woman, a gracious host, an expert businesswoman; now she seemed pitiful, broken almost. She almost felt sorry for her. Almost, but not quite. "So who is this guy?" she demanded.

"Do you want to hear the whole story, or would you rather have short answers to start with?"

Courtney sat back on the couch. "I guess you might as well just tell me the whole story."

Grace remained perched on the edge of the couch, unable to look at Courtney as she recounted the events that had taken place so many years ago.

"Okay, well as you know, Lucy was what my parents thought of as their miracle baby. I'd come along, and then they had tried and tried for years for more children with no luck. I think they had all but given up when Mom found herself pregnant almost seven years later.

"They thought of her as a real gift from God and felt truly blessed. It was just as well they had started trying for a family straight away, or else Mom might have been too old and Lucy might never have come along.

"The Ballantynes were friends of the family and highly respected members of our community and church. Their son, Zac, was only a year older than Lucy, so they were members of some of the same youth groups, shared classes and activities at school.

"They more or less grew up together. When they reached their teens, everyone had hopes of them dating, and they weren't disappointed. They'd been inseparable from about the age of twelve anyway. They made a lovely couple and they were very much in love." Grace smiled softly at the memories.

"She used to call me up after every date and we would spend hours talking on the phone, going over every detail of them. I was a couple of years older than she was, but I hadn't forgotten that magical time of the first stirrings of love. We used to talk and giggle like best friends. My baby sister was completely in love and I didn't have any doubts they would end up together."

"So what happened?"

"Zac and Lucy were very young, and after courting a while, they were unable to follow the teachings of the church. I was just twenty-three by this time, graduated, married and living in a small house with John and Carrie and the newborn twins. She called me up one evening, sobbing her heart out."

"Don't tell me, she was pregnant!" Courtney interjected bitterly.

"Well, she'd missed two periods and was terrified. She didn't know what to do. I left John with the kids and headed straight over to get her, making some excuse to our parents. I can't even remember what it was. I tried to calm her down that night, told her not to worry until we knew for sure. She eventually cried herself to sleep in my arms.

I told her the next morning to go to school as normal, pretend everything was okay just for a little while longer. I went into town and bought a pregnancy testing kit from the pharmacy. I got a few comments about how after having three so quickly, I should know by now, but other than that, nobody really thought much about it, which meant there was no gossip. If Lucy had done it, it would have been all over town within a few hours no doubt. Anyway, I had hoped it was just a false alarm … teenage hormones, you know?"

Courtney nodded and shrugged her agreement with the premise at least. She understood Grace could have saved Lucy a lot of embarrassment and shame if the test had been negative.

"So, she stayed over the next night, we did the test and the results were positive. I know these things aren't always reliable, but we were fairly certain it was right. There was nothing else to do; we had to tell Mom and Dad. I took her home in the morning instead of taking her to school, announcing that we needed to speak to them. As you can imagine, they were pretty horrified, but they were very supportive too, once they had gotten over the shock. Lucy was only sixteen; she was still their little miracle and she would need all the help she could get. They were sure that Zac loved her and his parents would agree to them getting married as soon as possible.

"I had married at eighteen and was expecting Carrie when I was nineteen and I was blissfully happy; there was nothing to suggest this couldn't have a happy ever after for them, too. They invited the Ballantynes over that evening to discuss it. Unfortunately, it didn't go as well as they had hoped. The

Ballantynes were furious, calling Lucy every name under the sun, saying she had tempted their son and lead him astray.

Zac, who had turned 17 by then, tried to fight them, begged them to let him marry Lucy, but they stormed out, dragging him with them, saying he was never to see her again. Three days later, the Ballantynes moved away, telling no one and leaving no forwarding address. And, of course, taking Zac with them. Lucy never saw or heard from him again."

"Surely you must have tried to find him?"

Grace shook her head. "We didn't have access to the resources we have today, remember? Also, Lucy said that Zac knew where she was, and that if he loved her, if he cared about her and his unborn child at all, he would have found a way to get in touch. She said if he didn't want to be involved, she would never make him."

"Makes sense I guess. I think I would have said the same."

"Lucy was independent and stubborn, just like you," Grace smiled.

"So what happened next?"

"Lucy stayed at home for awhile, and then when the baby was almost due, she asked if she could move in here with us. She had various reasons. I think she felt it would be less shameful for Mom and Dad if she weren't living at home. In addition, the environment here was very baby-oriented what with my lot running around, and we had Maggie to help. I think she was very scared of the labor, of looking after something so vulnerable by herself, just the whole thing really. I can imagine it would be pretty terrifying at that age; it was hard enough at nineteen.

"I thought it was a great idea and I spoke to John. Of course, he agreed straight away and she moved in, and you came along pretty soon afterwards. With hindsight, I also think that she wanted to live here because it was more isolated. She more or less cut herself off from people, never could face going back to church, atoning, and making amends. She gave birth to a beautiful baby girl that we all adored. For three months, things were fine and it looked like everyone had come to terms with the situation. Your cuteness helped with that a lot.

"Although Lucy didn't want to go, she wanted you raised in the church and begged me to take you with us when you were older. All that changed about a month later when she came home one day after a rare trip into town full of talk about some cowboy she had met. Within two weeks, she had packed up all her belongings and moved in with David Fisher."

"Didn't anyone try to stop her?"

"Of course we begged her to reconsider, to give it more time. We hadn't even met the man; we might have tried even harder if we had. Just before she left, she came to me, pleading with me to understand.

"Although she seemed quite happy and content, she really couldn't handle the shame of being a single mom at her age. She was desperate to move to another town and start anew as a married woman, and this man was willing to marry her and adopt you. How could I deny her that? I backed her up; helping her convince everyone that it was the right thing to do."

A single tear ran down Grace's cheek. "I know now it was the worst thing I could have done, especially for you. When he demanded that we stay away from you and her, we didn't fight too hard, because I couldn't bear to see what my actions had led to. I was a coward, Courtney, and I'm sorry. I should have been there every day, trying to convince her to leave him and come home."

Courtney could understand where Grace was coming from, how torn and conflicted she had been. It made sense that she would stand by her sister and fight for what she wanted. Even staying away made sense. She knew that Lucy would have asked her to, to avoid trouble and keep the peace with her new husband. She didn't doubt that Grace had done what she felt was right and with the best of intentions. None of that had been her fault, but she wasn't ready to let Grace off the hook completely.

"I don't blame you for any of that, nor do I think you were a coward. What was cowardly though, was not telling me all this sooner. Why, Grace?"

Grace gulped and carried on, knowing that this was too late, but that she had to confess everything to Courtney. "After Lucy died and David fell to pieces, we knew that we had to get you out of there. Although I didn't have much contact with Lucy over the years, that changed a lot in the final months of her illness. She told me how David treated you, how he had never really taken to you or considered you his own. I'm sorry, but the truth has been concealed for too long. He wanted a son, but Lucy couldn't have any more children after you. She'd been so young and the birth was complicated. He resented you a lot.

"After you'd been with us a few months and he hadn't even made contact, we knew for sure he didn't care. He was lost in the bottom of a bottle. We consulted an attorney who advised us that because he had legally adopted you when you were a baby, his signature was all we needed if we wanted to apply for guardianship.

"We had no need to contact your real father," Grace continued. "David had no problem signing the forms. It seemed like he couldn't wait to give up responsibility for you. After you had been with us for a year, it seemed like a natural progression to adopt you fully, and the process was easy since David didn't protest and you were happy with us."

"Do you remember that woman that arrived with a tape recorder and a clipboard and sat and spoke to you for about two hours?"

"Yes, I remember."

"She was an *ad lidem* attorney for the court, appointed to represent your interests before the court. She was trying to determine if you were happy and cared for, if you missed your father, and so forth. She reported that it was in your best interest for the adoption to proceed.

Once you were legally adopted, you had a complete new set of papers, a new last name, and the whole thing has been locked away in this box ever since. Oh Courtney, I meant to tell you. At first, you were too young and too fragile after losing your mother. When you finally settled in, it was so good to see you happy that I didn't want to disrupt you all over again. Then you started your teen rebellion, sneaking out, drinking, hanging out with boys, parking with them …"

"You knew about all that?" Courtney was shocked.

"Of course I did. This is a close knit community, and things don't take long to get back, sometimes with good intentions, sometimes not so much."

"So why didn't you say anything?"

"You'd been through so much, I thought the behavior was just a reaction to it all. I figured you would work it all out of your system eventually. You were so smart and tough and you had a sensible head on your shoulders. I never believed you would ever get into serious trouble. I let it all go, leaving you to work through it, trusting you to find your own way. But you can see why I felt it still wasn't the right time to tell you, right? I was afraid it would push you away from us even more, send you off the rails completely."

Courtney ran her hand through her hair. "Yeah, I guess I can see that, but what about later?"

Grace looked miserably at Courtney. "I guess I kept making excuses to myself. You had finally settled down, you were busy with your exams and studies. You were doing so well at your new job in the firm. There just always seemed to be a reason not to tell you, not to interfere with the life you had built. Then it just seemed too late, like the moment had passed and I had missed my chance. I felt that if I told you now, it would create a divide between us. You'd think I'd lied to you, kept things from you."

"That's exactly what I think."

"I know. All I can say is I'm sorry. Maybe one day you will understand why I did it and perhaps find it in your heart to forgive me."

"Who else knows?"

"Only me, David and the solicitor who handled the paperwork, if they're still around. John and Lucy were the only other two who ever knew."

"I'm going for a ride."

Courtney didn't even glance in Grace's direction as she rose and marched from the room, slamming the door behind her.

Chapter Eight

Out of consideration for her dear friend, who was getting on in years, Courtney didn't saddle Ice when she got to the stables. She wanted to ride hard, to use speed and risks to whisk her rage from her mind. Instead, she saddled a horse that only John and the stable hands ever rode, a jet-black stallion that was named Knight, though Courtney secretly nicknamed him Demon. He was all fire and passion, perfect for how she wanted to ride today.

She ignored the protests of the stable groom, who begged her to choose a different horse, a safer one. She mounted the horse and broken the rules by urging him into a gallop while still in the stable, his hooves kicking up a shower of gravel as they flew across the yard, not stopping to open the gate. She gave the mighty beast his head, feeling him quiver in excitement as the high fence and gate came into view.

She laughed with delight as they soared over it, landing in the adjoining paddock and scattering the other horses who grazed there. Onward they rode, jumping every obstacle that blocked their relentless path. Only when Demon was puffing heavily and had a sheen of sweat over his black coat did she slow down his pace, wondering if she exorcised any of her own demons in the process.

Slowing her horse to a walk to allow him to cool down, she felt the overwhelming urge to talk things over with someone, but not just anyone, she wanted to talk to Peter. Taking a chance on the fact that he might be home on a Saturday, she rode hard to his house, relieved when his family welcomed her and told her he was in the study.

She visited with them while she waited for him to finish up some paperwork he was working on, and while Demon was allowed a well-earned feed, water and rub down in the Anderson's stables. The minute Peter walked into the room, Courtney jumped to her feet.

"Will you ride with me?"

"Sure, just let me go and change, it looks a nice day for a ride."

Courtney sat back down and waited impatiently for Peter to reappear. Now, they sat by a small stream, the horses tethered nearby, munching contentedly on grass. She repeated the story told to her that morning, adding her own caustic additions in the recount. Peter listened, letting her rant, being everything a good friend should be. Now that the words had dried up, it was his turn to offer what words of wisdom he could.

"I understand it's a complete shock, and an injustice, but I can also understand Grace's point of view."

"You would."

"What's that supposed to mean?"

"Nothing I guess," Courtney muttered, unwilling to take her anger out on Peter, even though she felt like it. She leapt up from the ground and paced back and forth.

Peter laughed softly. "Courtney, you are a force to be reckoned with at the best of times, you are truly a sight to behold when you're angry!"

Courtney whirled to face him, hands on hips, eyes flashing. "This is no laughing matter, Peter Anderson!"

Peter instantly sobered. "I know that, but tell me what it is exactly that you're mad about."

"That so much of my life has been a lie," Courtney replied, returning to her pacing.

"Has it really been? Your mother loved you; Grace and John loved you and your cousins accepted you as a sister without question. There was only one lie ever told, and that was that David Fisher was your father. Even then, in a way he was as he'd legally adopted you. Are you upset that he isn't?"

Courtney threw up her hands in exasperation. "No! Why would I be, he's an ass, and a drunken ass at that, but so is my real father because he didn't fight for what he claimed to want and love. Why do things have to be this way? People I love leave me, then I find that other people I love lie to me and keep secrets from me, and now my own father didn't want me. Isn't there anyone out there I can trust and rely on?"

"Yes, there is, if only you'd open your heart to Him."

"Oh, don't you dare start in with the religious bullshit right now, Peter. I so do not want to hear it. My father was right in one thing: your lot aren't half as saintly as you pretend to be."

Peter sighed, seeing all the progress he had made over the months disappearing. "I don't think any of us claim to be saintly, we just try to be the best people we can be. We're all human, and that means that we make mistakes, lose our way sometimes. As long as we learn from those mistakes and let Him guide us back on our path, we deserve to be given another chance. I understand you're mad at Grace for not telling you, but don't you think she has agonized over that decision, prayed about it every night, trying to find the right thing to do?"

"Well, she obviously didn't get an answer because she chose wrong."

"I can see how it seems that way at the moment," Peter replied, nodding.

"I get the feeling you wanted to add a 'but' on the end of that sentence. Out with it."

"Only if you come back and sit down."

Courtney did as she was asked, flopping down beside Peter. "Come on then, explain to me why I'm wrong to be angry."

"I'm not saying you're wrong. All I'm saying is that I think Grace made a few valid points that are worth your consideration. I remember when I first met you; you were so lost, so alone. I can see that Grace made the right choice not to tell you once you had finally settled in and accepted the Carpenters as your new family, I'd have made the same decision."

"Yeah, maybe," Courtney conceded. "But that was years ago, she's still had all this time."

"Obviously she was afraid."

"Afraid of what?"

"You acting like this."

Courtney groaned and dropped her head into her hands. "This is all such a mess."

"Not really, when you think about the bigger picture. Everything that happened was a long time ago, it's over with and everybody has moved on. It's only you that needs to catch up. As far as David Fisher is concerned, he's no loss at all. In fact, I would have thought it would be good to be free of any responsibility for him. In terms of Grace, well, doesn't she deserve some compassion and forgiveness for this small misjudgment? Doesn't everything she has done for you prove she loves you and acted with the best intentions?"

"You know what, as annoying as it is, you're right. This isn't Grace's fault, and although I would have preferred that it had come from her, I'm glad I know now and she was honest with me eventually. I know she loves me, and I love her too, as much as I love my real mom. I'll never forget everything this family did for me, does for me, and I'd be an ungrateful little brat if I threw it all back in their faces over something like this."

"Wouldn't be the first time."

"For what?" Courtney asked absently, already planning her apology to Grace for her earlier actions.

"For being an ungrateful little brat."

"Why you!" Courtney leapt on Peter and slapped at him playfully.

They wrestled together and Peter easily flipped her, ending up sitting on her chest with her arms pinned to the ground. He looked down at her laughing face and his gaze softened. "You are so beautiful," he whispered.

Courtney's laughter faltered in her throat and she stared back up at Peter, her lips parting slightly in a subconscious request. Peter bent his head slowly towards her, making his intent clear, giving her time to refuse. Courtney held still, her heart racing and her lungs desperate for more air.

As Peter's lips met hers in a firm, masculine press, her senses exploded and she responded eagerly with growing passion as the kiss lengthened and deepened. Her body was on fire as she tasted his mouth, smelled his masculine scent mixed with the fresh, tangy cologne he used, felt the softness of his hair as he released her arms and she ran her fingers through it. She wrapped her arms around his back, pulling him deeper into the kiss.

Courtney couldn't help herself; finally, she felt what she had only ever read about, and while in the arms of a real man. She began to writhe against him. Peter pulled away, flinging himself off her and laying by her side panting, his reaction to her plainly obvious for her to see, thrilling her and exciting her further.

"Courtney, we can't."

Courtney turned on her side to face him, running her fingers across his chest. "Why not, nobody would know."

"I would know, and He would know," Peter replied, grabbing her fingers as they began to move lower. "Please don't, you're testing my resolve to the max as it is."

"I want you to forget all about your resolve."

"You might think you do, here and now and in the heat of passion, but I know you, you'd feel guilty and ashamed afterwards."

"I don't think I would, I would feel wonderful, amazing, fulfilled and sated and …"

"Courtney, just stop it, it can't happen. I can't deny I want you right now, but you know how important my church and its teachings are to me. Making love to you would be all those things, but it would also be against everything I believe in, and I just can't do it, as much as my body is telling me otherwise."

Courtney flung herself back onto her back and sighed. "Guess I'm just not woman enough for you, huh?"

It was Peter's turn to roll over and face her, his head resting on his hand. "Courtney, you are everything I could ever want in a woman. You're beautiful; you're sexy, sassy, cheeky, intelligent, quick-witted, funny and interesting. You captured my imagination and my heart from the very first day I met you. For years, you were my best friend and I loved you. I still love you and I think I'll always love you."

"I love you too, Peter, you're still my best friend," Courtney replied, giving him a quick, non-erotic hug before leaping to her feet. "Thanks for listening to me and talking me down, on both matters. I guess we should get home. I have some fences to mend."

"Would those be all the ones you knocked down with that crazy horse?"

Courtney chuckled, but it was an uneasy laughter. Now that the moment of passion had passed, she felt a little awkward and embarrassed by her reaction to the kiss. She still didn't really understand why he kissed her in the first place; he had never shown any romantic intentions toward her. She knew that dating would be futile; it could never lead to anything more since she wasn't a member of his church. As she mounted her horse, she decided she must have invited him with her body language, and Peter being Peter, had given in to what she wanted. It was her fault, and it was up to her to get over it.

"I'll have you know that Demon here is an excellent jumper, we cleared everything in our path," she said with fake indignation, leaning forward to stroke the horse's neck.

"Demon," Peter snorted as he swung into the saddle of his own mount. "I guess it's an appropriate nickname for him. You should be more careful though, I thought only John and Simon could handle him. Even Carter would never ride Knight."

"Maybe, but he's met his match in me," Courtney grinned, some of the awkwardness leaving as she bantered with Peter. Even as she spoke, she could feel the tension in the horse below her, his muscles quivering with barely reigned in power and desire to be free. Knowing she needed to tire the horse once more, she scanned the horizon. "Race you to that tree line," she yelled, urging Knight into a gallop, leaving Peter scrambling for his reins.

Courtney whooped and laughed as Knight flew over the ground, his hooves pounding, the scenery around them blurring with their speed. She urged him on, leaning close over his neck, leaving the reins slack in her hand.

She wasn't at one with this horse, but she felt she knew his mind regardless. All he wanted was for his speed to dislodge his annoying rider and confining tack, to be rid of the things that constrained him and to run wild, forever free.

There were no loving whickers and gentle nudges from this one, the most she would ever gain was a grudging respect for staying on his back, and even that was doubtful. Courtney laughed again and the horse flared his nostrils in annoyance. As they approached the tree line, she gathered up the reins firmly and began to pull him up, slowing his pace. He shook his head in annoyance and danced sideways as they came to a slow walk.

Courtney turned him to look for Peter, prepared for Knight to rear or buck at any moment. To her surprise, Peter wasn't quite as far behind as she thought he would be. It only took about five minutes for him to reach her side, the presence of his horse settling down her Demon ride.

"He might be a high-strung idiot, but he's pretty fast," Peter admitted as he looked at the horse. "But I still can't understand why John took him on."

"Oh, the usual John type of thing," Courtney grinned. "He'd had three owners, none of which could handle him. He didn't have a future until John heard about him."

Peter nodded. "Yep, that sounds like John, always taking in the wild, untamable strays."

He looked pointedly at Courtney and raised one eyebrow.

"Hey!" she laughingly protested. "Just for that I should make you swap on the ride home."

"No way," Peter shivered. "I like my neck how it is, in one piece."

"Chicken."

"You bet."

They continued to banter as they headed home, Courtney insisting that she see Peter home first. She wanted some time alone to consider how she was going to approach Grace and apologize to her. She also wanted to explain her earlier actions, hoping they could both see each other's point of view and move on from their earlier discord. She knew she had hurt Grace; now it was time to make it up to her in any way she could.

Chapter Nine

Courtney was finding it hard to concentrate on the words before her. She had long since made up with Grace, but the subject kept nagging at her, buzzing around in her head like an annoying wasp at a picnic.

She didn't really have anyone to talk to about it. She didn't want to raise the subject with Grace again - her sister's unhappiness, early passing and the choices Grace had made were obviously painful for her to relive. Despite being reassured to the contrary, Grace still blamed herself for not doing more to help Lucy and Courtney.

Courtney also felt guilty running to Peter every time she had a problem. Lately, all she seemed to do was whine to him about one thing or another. She would have gladly talked things over with Chelsea but on their return from their honeymoon, she and Kade moved into a gorgeous little two-bedroom cottage that the Richardson's and Grace had jointly bought for their wedding gift. She knew her sister would take time out to meet with her if she asked, but she was so busy working, decorating, and turning the cottage into a home. Besides, she was a newlywed; she didn't need to be dealing with someone else's drama.

Courtney thought over the current family situation. Carrie and Antonio had gone back to their lives in New York City, combining their apartments; Carter was in San Francisco; Chelsea had moved in with Kade, although she wasn't far away. That left only her and Cassie at home, but Cassie lived in the guesthouse, saying she needed the peace and privacy to write. She had turned the top floor of the house into a large office, and that's where she spent most of her time. She thought Cassie would have moved away from home by now.

I think I've proven myself enough that Grace would agree to a transfer to any of the various company offices, or maybe even allow me to open a brand new branch somewhere, if only I would ask.

Being the only one left living at home should spur me on to make the move, yet somehow I don't think I'm ready. Part of it is because of Grace. How would she feel left alone in this huge house haunted by memories of a large, happy family? She has

Maggie and Nigel of course, but they go to their little home every night. No, it was too soon after Chelsea leaving for me to go, too. Her relief at coming to this conclusion made her admit that Grace's feelings were only a small part of it. After recently being reunited with Peter, she wasn't ready to leave him either.

She threw down the manuscript she was working on, knowing she wasn't going to get anything done until she let her thoughts play out. She spent hours reliving that kiss with Peter by the river.

She knew she had loved him as a friend, and she'd been attracted to him the minute she had seen him again, all grown up. It hadn't taken her that long to admit to herself that she loved him as more than a friend.

Her plan to ignore it and make it go away hadn't worked at all. The more often she saw him, the stronger her reaction was to his presence. Whenever she wasn't with him, she longed for his company and wanted to talk over every tiny aspect of her life with him.

If it had been a while since she had seen him, she felt bereft and lost; the same way she felt each time they parted company, no matter how long they had spent together. All those things, combined with her instant reaction to him calling her beautiful and kissing her, could add up to only one thing: she didn't just love him, she was completely and utterly head over heels *in love* with him.

"Well, that kind of complicates things, doesn't it?" she muttered to the empty office as if a response would bounce off the walls right back at her.

She didn't know if her feelings were reciprocated. She knew Peter loved her as a friend, he had told her so on many occasions. There could be no doubt that he had responded to her; she had clearly seen that impressive evidence! She grinned to herself wickedly at the memory, tempted to pick up events and continue them in her imagination. *Stop it!* She told herself firmly, this is no time for rampant fantasies.

During the wedding, Antonio had hinted that she and Peter should have attended as a couple, that Peter couldn't take his eyes off her the whole night. That was the end of her actual evidence and facts, and it wasn't quite enough to come to the conclusion that Peter might feel the same way for her as she did for him. *Even if he did feel that way, we couldn't be together unless I was willing to take some action; I'd need to become an active member of the Mormon faith. Odds are that Peter would never settle for less than a marriage in the temple where couples are sealed for time and eternity. He says he would never be married in a civil ceremony where they say, "Till death do you part."*

She leaned back in her chair, considering how she felt about that. *What a huge step that would be for me after I've spent my whole life refusing to go to church with the family.* Her father had nothing but bad things to say about them and her mom actually leaving the church seemed to back this up. Her earliest views of the faith had been colored by David's hatred before she even learned anything about them or even met an active member outside the Carpenter family.

Losing her mom at such a young age had done nothing to help remedy that. She could even recall a few times she had verbally denied the existence of a God at all. She hadn't really believed that, but she had been angry, confused and lost. She had felt forsaken and abandoned, and she'd wallowed in self-pity, raging against anyone who tried to tell her she was loved and that there were reasons for why she was made to experience the things she had.

Giving it deeper thought, she admitted that she admired the Carpenter's values, and for the most part, apart from her coffee addiction and a few naughty thoughts, she mostly lived by them herself, without really making a conscious effort to do so. She had been quite excited by the thought of Peter being a returning missionary, although she hadn't understood why. It held a certain prestige of course, but it was also kind of sexy too, in an odd way that she couldn't quite fathom.

In the many hours they had spent discussing things, he had spoken a lot about paths, lessons and spiritual growth. It had made a lot of sense to her and admittedly, when he spoke, she felt soothed inside, as if her anger was lifted from her, leaving her with a sense of peace. She also recalled how easily it had come to her to explain things to the Dominguez family, and how she had defended the wedding guests against David Fisher's accusations.

Maybe it wasn't such a stretch after all to imagine herself as part of this faith. Picking up the phone, she decided she needed to talk to the one person she knew that had been through this, that had probably had the same doubts and fears she had but had come through them. Dialing the number, she listened to the phone ring in New York, hoping Antonio was at home.

It was nearly two hours later that she replaced the receiver, thinking what a wonderful man her sister married. Just like Peter, he was understanding, patient and extremely generous with his time, eager to help her out. During the long and intense call, he gently asked her some probing and personal questions, which she tried to answer in the most upfront and honest manner she could. He was delighted to inform her that the beliefs she already held made up a large part of the Mormon faith.

He laughingly told her that all she needed was a little fine-tuning and some help with the day-to-day rules that she would need to follow to be temple worthy. He eased her mind about whether she would be doing it for the right reasons, explaining that since she already believed, loved and respected God, there could be no wrong reason for taking steps to become closer to Him, or for choosing a particular method to show Him how much she wanted and needed Him in her life.

Courtney chuckled to herself; it was almost like talking to Peter, but considering it was Peter who had brought Antonio into the faith through his missionary teaching, that shouldn't have surprised her. She could hear for herself how much Antonio now loved this faith, despite his conversion from a devout Catholic to Mormon. She herself had never really been anything except a believer. If Antonio could make such drastic changes with no regrets, then surely she could too.

There was one small matter that might hold her back. Right now, with her recent discovery, she felt a little lost, as if her identity was snatched away from her. She wasn't who she thought she was anymore. How could she embark on a new direction if she had no concept of half her heritage? No, before she could even begin to devote herself to a religion and hand her heart and soul into the hands of God for safekeeping, she needed to truly know for herself where she had come from. She had to find her biological father.

With the decision made, Courtney could now go back to work, her mind finally settled on the path ahead.

Chapter Ten

That night, in the privacy of her bedroom, Courtney booted up her laptop and opened her browser. She typed in the name that occupied her thoughts, not really sure what she was hoping to find. Within less than a second, her search engine declared it had found over 350,000 results for the name Zachary Edward Ballantyne. A quick glance at the results on the first page told her she could be there for hours trying to sift through the information and perhaps not find anything useful.

Clearing the name, she tried again, using the way someone had signed the document instead of how the hospital clerk had filled in the birth certificate. The results for Zachary E. Ballantyne were better, only one hundred and seventy-six thousand this time. Studying the first page, she discovered that most of them were social media links. With a sigh, she began to open them up and take a look.

Twenty minutes later after viewing several teenage profiles and twenty-something entrepreneurial freelance business promotions, she realized she was being silly. She didn't have the paperwork; she wasn't sure what happened to the box when she stormed out. It was gone from the coffee table when she returned and she hadn't wanted to ask Grace about it again. She did, however, remember that she had said her father was less than a year older than her mom, meaning she could pinpoint his year of birth down to two possible years.

Adding the first option to the name, she refreshed the search. Well, it was a step in the right direction having narrowed the results to just over thirty thousand, but it was still a daunting task, especially when she had no idea how to confirm anything even if she could locate a likely candidate. She really needed more information, or a genius at genealogy. She didn't have either, but she did know someone who really knew her way around internet research. She shut down her laptop and headed out the door, heading over to the guesthouse.

Cassie greeted her enthusiastically as she answered the knock at the door.

"Oh, thank you, I was so ready for a break and you're the perfect excuse, come on in."

It was easy for Courtney to see that her sister had been working. She was dressed in scruffy jeans and a faded top, barefooted, and her thick mane of short, dark brown hair was a disheveled mess. Her sister had a habit of abusing it when she was writing, twirling and chewing strands when she was thinking, running clawed fingers through it when she was frustrated, fluffing it up before diving back in to her imaginary world the same way someone would crack their fingers and flex their muscles before lifting weights at a gym.

Her shiny locks always ended up a tangled mess resembling a bird's nest by the end of every day. The family teased her about it constantly, but they were habits she just couldn't break, probably wasn't even aware of doing them at the time.

"Thanks, I was hoping it was late enough for you to call it quits. I really want to talk to you about something."

"Ohhh, sounds serious, should I make some hot chocolate?"

"A beer or a glass of wine would appeal more, but since they're not an option, I'll settle for the hot chocolate."

Cassie made her way to the kitchen and Courtney followed, taking a seat at the breakfast bar and watching her sister as she began to break up pieces of chocolate into a bowl.

"So what's up?" Cassie asked over her shoulder as she filled the kettle and put it on to boil.

"I made a discovery recently; I'm not sure whether Grace has mentioned anything, or if you maybe already knew."

"About what?" Cassie asked breezily as she filled a pan with boiling water and placed the bowl of chocolate on top to melt.

"About my father."

"David? I heard he had to be escorted off the premises. Sorry Courtney, that must have been pretty bad for you."

"Not him, about my real father."

Cassie turned to look at Courtney, her confused expression telling her she knew nothing about the things that had been said that night, or the subsequent conversation with Grace. Courtney was partially relieved that Grace had maintained the confidentiality, but also disheartened that she would have to go through it all again, reliving the emotions of the revelations.

"Let's wait until the drinks are ready then I'll start from the beginning," Courtney sighed.

An hour later, they were in Cassie's upper floor office, made by knocking out a wall to combine two rooms into one and turning it into a bright, dual-aspect space, ideal for working long hours. They sat together on the old, battered sofa that Cassie had installed for moments when she needed to take a rest away from her desk. Courtney proceeded to tell her the whole story, beginning at the wedding reception and right up to her conversation with Antonio and subsequent decision, although she kept her reasons for considering joining the faith to herself for the moment.

"Wow, that's some story; you couldn't write this stuff could you?"

"Well, you probably could," Courtney replied sassily.

"Nice to see you haven't lost your sense of humor," Cassie replied, sticking her tongue out at Courtney. "I'm not really sure which parts to address first. To be honest, I'm glad David Fisher isn't your dad. Your real dad might be a creep for making no effort to get in touch, but he can't be as bad as him."

"I agree, but I don't think it matters. It's more about knowing where I come from, reconciling myself with that. If it turns out he's a serial killer or something, then at least I'll know my genetic tendencies."

Cassie looked at Courtney with raised eyebrows. "Yes, I could actually see that being the case."

"Hey!"

The girls laughed and Courtney had to admit it felt good. Being wrapped in the arms of this family was the best thing that had ever happened to her, and right now, she appreciated it more than anything else in the world. Even if Cassie couldn't help her, it was so good to talk this over.

"I think I see where you're coming from, although it's hard to put into words. If you're uncertain about the past, how can you move forward with any certainty in the future?"

"Exactly, I just knew you'd get it, Sis."

"So how can I help?"

"I'm not sure if you can. Do you remember the Ballantynes at all?"

Cassie screwed up her face then shook her head. "I'm sorry, I don't. I'm only two years older than you are, I barely remember Aunt Lucy living with us. It would really be Carrie you would need to ask since she's the oldest. I really like saying that, you know?" And they both laughed.

"I didn't want to drag everyone into it. I just really wanted to do some clandestine hunting around and see what I could find."

"You think I can help with that?"

"I'm sure you can. How many hours do you spend researching stuff online, finding those perfect, obscure little details that give everything you write that ring of truth and believability, ensuring your readers become truly invested in the characters and forget they are reading a story?"

"Quite a few I guess," Cassie conceded. "What are we waiting for? I love 'clandestine.' Let's get started!"

Four hours later, the girls had narrowed things down to six likely candidates, although they had no way to tell for sure if Courtney's biological father even had an internet presence at all. It could be none of these, or someone they had discarded earlier. Cassie ran her fingers through her locks, sighing. "You know this would be a lot easier if you'd just talk to Grace again."

"Don't you think she'd be upset if she knows I'm looking? Isn't that kind of like a slap in the face after all she's done for me?"

"Not if you explain it right, no. I don't think she'll take it like that at all. Don't you realize how happy we would be if you really did consider joining the church? Not that we don't love you anyway, of course, but it would be so nice to share those things with you after all these years. I was so excited about that part, but I've been trying to play it down and focus on the father issue. I really want to get up and dance around the room."

"You played it down pretty well. I'm impressed." Courtney replied. "You know what? I hadn't thought about that making any difference to you guys, only me. How selfish is that? Perhaps I'm not cut out for it after all."

Cassie pealed with laughter. "Courtney, you have spent your whole life not changing for anyone, refusing for your own reasons. Why would you consider it selfish now to think only of yourself when actually considering doing something that would delight us all?"

Courtney grinned sheepishly. "I don't know, when you put it like that it does sound pretty silly. I guess I'm trying to learn a new way of thinking, trying to examine my every action and judge it more harshly."

"You don't get to judge, Courtney. That's what you need to learn. Hand yourself over to Him and He'll guide you every step of the way. You won't be second-guessing your every action and thought anymore. He'll teach you and you'll learn and grow with Him by your side. It really is awesome."

"Thanks, I'll keep that in mind."

"So what's next?"

"I don't know; shall we see if any of the candidates for fatherhood have social media pages with lots of pictures?"

"Sure, it'll be fun, even if it doesn't get us any further."

Fifteen minutes later, the girls were staring at the screen in silence. Cassie's hand still rested on her mouse, having used her more powerful desktop rather than her laptop for the search. The images in front of them showed a smiling man with two young girls at his side. His blond, floppy hair and chocolate eyes were practically a mirror image of Courtney's own.

"It couldn't be, could it?" Cassie whispered, wondering if Courtney was seeing what she was seeing.

"Could be coincidence, dark brown eyes aren't exactly rare."

"Yah, but they're your *exact* shade and the hair even looks like the same texture. He's around the right age, and look at the park bench. If the perspective isn't deceiving, he's not that tall, only about 5 feet 8 or 9 inches. That would explain where you got your pixie gene."

"Ha, ha, very funny. Look at the location, Cassie, he lives in Orem."

"Goodness, that's just south of here through the Provo Canyon, probably only about 30 minutes' drive from here. Do you think he could have been that close all this time, that the Ballantynes only went as far as Orem?"

"Who knows, they might have moved to West Virginia for all we know, just because he lives here now doesn't mean a thing, but if they stayed in the same state then he's an even bigger moron for not staying in touch with Lucy. Besides, this could all be idle speculation. We have nothing to prove that this is the guy."

Cassie nodded then looked away from the picture on the screen to look into her sister's eyes. "Well, we could shut down and spend the rest of our lives wondering if we actually found him on the first night we looked, or we could print out the picture and take it to Grace."

"Oh come on, she hasn't seen him for over twenty years, she's not going to know."

"He was just seventeen when she last saw him, how much do guys change?" Cassie shrugged. "We could hunt through the albums and see if there are earlier photos, take a selection over to her?"

"You mean like a lineup? I hope he's not a criminal." They laughed.

Courtney stood up and paced around the room, confused by how fast things seemed to be moving. This was huge. She really hadn't expected to get anywhere so soon and be faced with it so suddenly. Now she wasn't sure she really wanted to go through with it after all.

"Courtney, I know what you're thinking. Look, what harm can it do to know one way or another? All he is right now is a profile on Facebook. You can walk away from it, you can read it and learn as much about him as you can from what's on here, or you can take it further if you want. You don't have to decide right now, but if we don't even find out if it's him, you don't even have those options."

"Yeah, you're right. Go for it then."

With a handful of freshly printed pages in a folder, the girls headed back to the main house, hoping that Grace hadn't gone to bed. Courtney knew if she was going to do this, she needed to do it fast before she lost her nerve. Walking into the family room, they found Grace sitting quietly reading a book. She looked up and smiled as they entered.

"Hi, girls. Cassie, to what do we owe this honor? Have you run out of food or is it clean clothes you need?"

"Not funny, Mom. I do visit for other reasons you know," Cassie grinned at her Mom, knowing she did take liberties with the main house but that Grace really didn't mind. "Courtney wants to discuss something important with you, I'm here as backup."

Courtney glared at her sister. She had deliberately given her the opening, but also no chance to back out. "Thanks for that, Cassie."

She took a seat on the couch across from Grace and Cassie sat by her side, ready to play mediator if this went badly. "The thing is … I've been doing a lot of thinking recently. Please understand that I love you all very much, you will always be my family and I'll be eternally grateful for all you've done for me but … well … umm … I feel as if I can't really move forward with my life until I reconcile myself with my past, know who I am exactly. Ever since I found out David wasn't my father, I've felt as if I'm not me anymore. Does that make any sense?"

Grace carefully placed her bookmark in her current page, closed her book, and leaned forward to lay it down on the coffee table. She smiled gently at Courtney. "Yes, it makes sense; in fact, I actually suspected it might be the case once you'd had time to think it over. You want to find your real father, don't you?"

Courtney breathed a sigh of relief, and love for her family welled up inside at the thought of how supportive they were being and how easy they were making it for her. "Yes I do. I mean, I don't know yet if I want to try to get in touch or anything. At the moment, I just want to know who he is, where he is, what kind of life he has, that sort of thing. I just need to get a sense of him, so I can have more of a sense of me."

"I understand what you're saying, but what I need you to remember is that no matter what, you will always be you,

Courtney. You are your own person and that can never change. Please don't lose sight of that through this journey."

"I'll try not to. Anyway, Cassie and I have been doing some research and we have come up with a few possibilities. We wanted to run them by you."

Grace took a deep breath. "Okay, but first, I have a confession to make. Please don't be mad at me Courtney, but when I considered this might happen, I did some research of my own. I knew who used to be close friends of the family and with whom they might have kept in touch. It was easy for me to find out where they went back then. Don't worry, I was very discreet and if you hadn't asked, I would have done nothing with the information, but I know a few things about your father."

Courtney was surprised and excited. The girls both scooted to the edge of the couch, anxious to hear more. Grace laughed at their eager expressions. "You remind me of when I used to read stories to you all, you were always on the edge of your seats back then, too.

"Okay, so they moved to Salt Lake City where Zac finished high school. From what I heard, he moved away from his parents as soon as he could. He enrolled at the John Hopkins University School of Medicine in Baltimore. He's now a pretty well-known heart surgeon working at the University of Utah Hospital in Salt Lake City.

"Once I knew that, I found lots of internet hits as his dissertations and studies are frequently published in medical journals and some of his patients are pretty high profile, either in the church, or in the political and sports worlds."

Courtney sat back, taking in the information. It wasn't so much the high profile heart surgeon that she struggled to wrap her head around; it was the fact that he was so close to her. She could take a short drive in the morning and possibly see her father for the first time. She shuddered at the thought, excited yet terrified. Pulling her attention back to the room, she watched as Cassie retrieved some of the pictures of the handsome man that had eyes so much like her own and handed them to Grace.

Grace's face softened as she looked at the pictures, a gentle smile curving her lips. "Yes, that's Zac. Apart from the laugh lines and the crow's feet, he hasn't changed that much. How did you find this?"

"Intrepid Researcher and Writer Extraordinaire," Cassie exclaimed proudly, causing them all to laugh. "Seriously though, we were working on guesswork and hunches until we saw this picture. Look at those eyes!"

"You always were the spitting image of him, Courtney. Lucy used to say that it got her through even the toughest times, looking at you and always seeing the only man she really loved looking back at her. Of course, it made it all the harder for David to accept you. When you were three years old, he found a photo album Lucy kept filled with pictures of her and Zac together. He was furious with her for keeping it, and he could never really look at you the same way again after that. I think he'd always known deep down that Lucy was still in love with Zac and not him, and you were a daily reminder for him."

"Poor Mom, she really didn't have a happy life."

"She had you, and that made her the happiest woman on this planet. You did really well finding this, girls. So we know where he works and what he looks like. What happens next?"

"We know from his profile that he lives in Orem. We could maybe narrow down the Ballantynes and find an address, then you could write to him," Cassie suggested. "Failing that, you could write to him at work."

"Oh sure, that would go down well. Opening his mail just before he goes into theatre and finding a letter from his daughter that he has never met and has made no effort to contact in twenty-three years," Courtney grumbled. "Shaky-handed surgeon anyone?"

Grace and Cassie couldn't help but laugh at Courtney, despite the magnitude of the situation. "Maybe it wasn't the best idea I've ever had," Cassie grinned sheepishly. "You could just private message him."

"I'm not so sure that social media would be correct etiquette for this sort of thing, Cassie. What do you think Courtney?"

"I think I need to give this time to sink in, and not rush into anything."

"Good plan, let's all go to bed and get some rest, we can regroup when Courtney feels ready," Grace said, standing and stretching. "Goodnight girls and good work."

The women all said goodnight and went their separate ways, Courtney knowing she was headed for a sleepless night.

Chapter Eleven

"This is pretty perfect. Well, as perfect as anything can be under the circumstances. Of course, I'm not convinced that the method of delivery is appropriate."

Peter handed her back the sheet of paper that Courtney had spent hours working on, draft after draft being discarded until she found what she felt were the correct words. The result was a short message that introduced herself as Lucy Carpenter's daughter and that if he would consider it, she would very much like to meet up and talk sometime. That was all it said.

As always, she wanted to run it past the one person who she completely trusted not to steer her wrong, the one person she wanted to share every part of her life with, Peter. It was Saturday so they had driven to town, just to hang out and spend the day together talking things over. They were currently in their favorite diner they had frequented since their early teens.

"Yeah, I know social media might not be the proper channels, but I think it's my best option."

"Listen, it seems like he's highly regarded in the church these days, teenage mistakes long forgiven and forgotten. Why don't you leave it with me? I'm sure that given a few days, I could find his address for you. I'm pretty well connected myself."

"I know you are, and you probably could, but I'm not sure if I want to know. What if I can't stop myself driving there, hanging around outside the house like some creepy stalker, or marching up to the door and demanding explanations?"

"For one, you have more self-control than that; two, you deserve some answers, he would understand that, and three, you're way too beautiful to be creepy," Peter grinned at her.

Courtney flushed. When Peter said things like that, she never knew how he meant them, could never decide if he was being funny, friendly, or even sarcastic. She had always considered herself a good judge of character and quick at assessing situations, but when it came to Peter, she was out of her league, blinded by her own hopes and fears.

"Don't bet on it," she replied. "I've already had to stop myself from driving to the hospital. The only reason I haven't is because the place is so big, I could be there for a month and never catch a glimpse of him."

"So you really want to meet him then."

Peter always hit upon what was in her heart, no matter what her sometimes smart mouth said. It was an uncanny knack of his that often left Courtney feeling open and exposed. "Yes, I've decided I really do, but what if he rejects me again?"

Peter reached over and took Courtney's hand in his, causing sparks of electricity to shoot through her and butterflies to dance in her tummy. "He didn't reject you; he was taken away from you. We have no idea what happened after that. Are you willing to give him the benefit of the doubt until you have the facts?"

Courtney had to admit that everything seemed better when she was with Peter. He put everything into perspective, had a unique way of looking at things that she loved. In short, he made the world a better place just by being in it.

"Of course I am; that's why I want to meet him, to hear what he has to say. Even if he doesn't want to meet, if he takes the time to explain his reasons I'll accept that. We know he has a family now and he might not want them to know about his past.

I do get that, but I'm just terrified that he simply ignores me completely, just shuns me and never replies."

"I can't promise you that it won't happen, but if it does it will be his loss. He has a chance to meet an amazing young woman of whom he should be proud, and he'd be a fool to pass it up. But if he does, you know I'll be here for you."

Courtney's heart leapt in her chest as he lifted her hand and gave her fingers a quick kiss before squeezing it reassuringly. *I love this man so much,* she thought. *He has no idea how much these small actions affect me. I wonder if they mean even half as much to him as they do to me.*

"Are you going to send it now?"

His question brought her back to the immediate problem. "I guess I should, it's the weekend after all, he might not be working and if I don't do it now, I'll lose my nerve."

Courtney reluctantly freed her hands from Peter's and dug her smartphone from her pocket, looking up Zac's profile on Facebook and hitting the 'send a message' box before she could chicken out. She typed the words that were on the piece of paper from memory, and then hesitated, suddenly unsure.

"I don't know if I can do this."

Peter calmly held out his hand and Courtney handed her phone to him, watching him hit the send button. She knew she would hand over her heart and soul to him just as easily, she trusted him so completely. "Thanks, so what now?"

"Now we forget about it and have a great day. Let's see what mischief we can get into." Peter grinned, tucking her phone into his pocket and rising from the booth, holding a hand out for her to join him.

Laughing, she took his offered hand and they headed out into the sunshine.

***

The movie credits rolled and Courtney felt rising trepidation as people around them began to file out of the cinema. They had decided to catch the late matinee, and she enjoyed a very nice two hours snuggled up against Peter who had wrapped an arm around her with easy affection. Now they would be leaving the darkness of the movie theatre and turning their cell phones back on, with no idea what might or might not be waiting for them.

As they reached the lobby and their eyes readjusted to the bright lights, Peter turned on the two phones. "You've got messages," he said casually. "Where do you want to go to read through them? Want to go for dinner?"

Courtney shook her head. "I've kind of lost my appetite right now."

"Okay, why don't we take a drive up to the temple grounds, it's beautiful up there, very calming and soothing for the soul. Listen, don't get your hopes up, there might not be a reply from him yet. Surgeons are pretty busy people you know, weekend or no weekend. You can't always plan your cardiac arrest for a working day."

"Your sense of humor is not helping right now."

"Well, I tried."

"You are very trying."

Cassie rolled her eyes at the quip. "An oldie, but always a goodie."

After the short drive, they walked to the fountain in the temple grounds, sitting down on a bench to admire the scenery around them.

"You're right, it is beautiful here."

Peter nodded and handed Courtney her phone. She flipped it over in her hands. "I can't do this; you look," she said, thrusting it back into his hands.

Peter nodded and opened up her social networking app, scrolling through the unread messages. "The one you're waiting for is definitely here. What do you want me to do?"

"I don't know. What do you think I should do?"

"Whatever you want."

"That doesn't help."

"Okay, okay, well the way I see it, you have only two choices. To read it, or not to read it. That is the question!"

She gave him a look … and a roll of her eyes. "Get serious!"

"Fifty-fifty, take your pick."

"So I could just delete it and forget this whole thing?"

"You could, but that would strike me as a little unfair considering you've probably just exploded this man's world, in a good way of course."

"So I don't really have a choice then?"

"I could offer another, read it now or read it later."

"Seems kind of dumb to put it off. Will you open it and read it first, maybe give me a heads up if it's really bad?"

"Sure, I can do that."

Courtney stared into Peter's face trying to pick up clues but he gave nothing away.

"It's not derogatory, insulting, rude or crude, do you want to hear it now."

Courtney's face broke into a grin. "You're teasing me now; you are, aren't you? You wouldn't do that if you weren't about to tell me something nice. Give me that phone!"

She grabbed for it but Peter held it out of her reach. "No way, I would have had to do the bad bit, so it's only fair I get to do the good bit. You hear about messengers getting shot, maybe this one will get a hug."

"Come on! Don't keep me in suspense any longer. What did he say?"

"Okay, here goes. Courtney, you have no idea how happy I am to hear from you. Would love to meet and talk. I'm free late afternoon tomorrow, any good for you?"

Courtney leapt from her seat and began dancing around in delight. She'd had no idea that this was the outcome she had really wanted, and badly, judging by her current giddiness.

"Do you want me to reply?"

"Of course, I do, silly man!"

"And what would you have me say?"

"Tell him yes," Courtney laughed as she spun and twirled at the fountain's edge, delighting in the burbling sound that made it seem as if the fountain was singing, celebrating along with her. She sat on the very edge, leaning in and plunging her hands into the glorious water, splashing it about in her joy and soaking herself in the process. "Yes, yes, yes!"

A reply came back almost instantly. "He's asking what time and where," Peter called to her.

A breathless and wet Courtney flung herself down next to Peter. "How about 4.30 p.m., right here."

Peter's thumbs flew over the onscreen keypad and the response in the affirmative came flying back. He locked her phone and handed it back to her. "Now that's all settled," he said, wrapping an arm around her. "Why don't we get some dinner, I'm ravenous? I'd been planning a nice restaurant, but looking at the state of you, I think we'd better make it the diner again. What were you going for, maybe a self-baptism?"

Courtney gave him a little punch. "Whatever, I don't mind."

"You know they're going to think we've taken up permanent residence? They'll be naming that table after us soon."

Their banter continued as they walked back to the car hand in hand. Once settled in the diner with their casual dinner, Peter looked at Courtney with an indulgent smile.

"Tell me what you're thinking. What exactly is it that's making you so happy about this situation?"

Courtney giggled. "To be honest, I'm not sure I really know. I guess it's a combination of things. I've been so uptight and confused since the wedding, so part of it is pure relief that all the uncertainty and not knowing is going to be resolved soon. Then of course, he didn't flat out tell me to get lost, so that's amazing. I'll get a chance to hear what happened back then and even if we hate each other or never want to see each other again, at least I'll know the full story and be able to come to terms with everything and put it to rest."

"I'm glad you have that attitude. When I saw you at the fountain I couldn't help but be worried that you were placing too much on this and might end up hurt or disappointed."

Courtney poked at her salad with her fork, her face turning serious. "No, I won't be disappointed, whatever happens, but I've felt almost in limbo recently, like I thought I knew who I was, and then suddenly I didn't. Even if someone is nothing like their parents, or doesn't want to be like their parents, I still feel it's really important to know your roots, where and what you come from. Am I making any sense at all?"

Peter nodded encouragingly and tried to smile around a massive mouthful of cheeseburger, his favorite indulgence. Courtney laughed again at his silly, beautiful face. "Anyway, I just feel that once this meeting is over, be it the first or last, I'll be able to move on and firm up some other major decisions I need to settle in my life. The fact that he wants to meet has just made everything seem possible, and the world and happiness are mine for the taking again."

"Courtney Carpenter out to conquer the world?"

"Exactly!"

"I'll drink to that," Peter said, raising his water glass for a toast.

Courtney happily obliged. "New beginnings," she added, before they clinked their glasses and drank.

Chapter Twelve

Courtney sat watching the beautiful display provided by the dancing water of the multiple jets of the fountain, the late afternoon sun causing it to sparkle like jewels. She glanced at her watch for the fifth time since her arrival, then stared morosely back at the water, unable to appreciate its brilliance today. Zac was already fifteen minutes late and she wondered if perhaps he had changed his mind and wasn't coming.

Peter had insisted on driving her here, claiming that it would be too emotional a day for her to risk being behind the wheel herself, that her full attention wouldn't be on the road. She'd had to concede that it made a lot of sense. She was comforted by the thought that he was waiting for her in town only a phone call and quick drive away, always there for her but giving her space to handle this on her own.

She looked up at the amazing architectural design of the temple itself. It was quite breathtaking, and Courtney shivered. It was an emotive place, but she couldn't quite reconcile her conflicting thoughts and feelings about it. It was soothing somehow, being here, and considering that this might be a large part of her future, exciting and thrilling. She also felt kind of intimidated by it, and guilty for being in the grounds in her uninitiated and ignorant state.

"It's a wondrous sight, isn't it?"

The gentle voice startled her and she leapt off the bench, turning to see a short and lean, but handsome man, standing there. "Zac?" she all but whispered.

"Yes, and you have to be Courtney."

She nodded mutely and they stared at each other, both looking into eyes that were a mirror image of their own. She felt completely overwhelmed by this situation, didn't know how to handle it, and wished she had asked Peter what she should do.

When Zac opened his arms, she flew into them without a moment's hesitation. He wrapped his arms around her tightly and held on as if he never wanted to let go. For a fleeting second, Courtney felt like a little girl again, with a Daddy who loved her and would take care of her, treating her like a princess. Suddenly feeling shy and awkward, she pulled away, surprised to see tears in Zac's eyes. He dipped his head and wiped them away, as if ashamed of his display. Her heart went out to him, realizing how hard this must be on him, too.

"Come and sit down and we'll chat for a bit. How was your journey?" she asked, hoping small talk would put them at ease.

"Oh, dreadful. I'm so sorry I'm late but little Jessie got really carsick. We had to stop and try to clean up the car, and let her change into a fresh outfit. Anything to get rid of the smell!"

"Oh no, that's awful. I'm sorry. I should have come to you and not put you to the trouble."

Zac shook his head. "Not at all, it's not your fault. We're hoping she'll grow out of it but in the meantime, we have to deal with it, and the more car journeys she has, maybe the quicker she'll get over it. We know what to pack for emergencies now."

"So Jessie's your daughter?"

"Yes, I have two other girls, Celeste, who's sixteen, and Jessie's eleven."

"I hadn't thought about you bringing them, where are they?"

"For the moment, they're having the time of their lives in town with Sandra, probably stuffing their faces with ice cream somewhere."

"Is that your wife?"

"Umm, no. Jessie was a difficult and complicated pregnancy, I'm afraid my wife, Jennifer, didn't make it through the birth. Sandra is kind of my live-in babysitter. I work long hours and can't always be there to pick them up from school or activities, so Sandra is their constant in life, always around when I can't be."

Courtney's hand flew to her mouth on hearing the news. "I'm so sorry for your loss."

"Thank you. It was terrible, but now I can look back on our time together and smile, and just be thankful that I didn't lose both of them."

They spent a few moments in contemplative silence, then Zac seemed to shake himself off and get his head back in the present moment. "Anyway, what I'm dying to know is all about you, Courtney. Where do we even start with all this?"

"How about the very beginning? It always seems like a good place to me."

He chuckled softly. "I guess it is. So tell me how much you already know and why now?"

Courtney could see them going around in circles and getting all tangled up, like struggling to find the end of a new ball of string or spool of thread. One of them needed to find a place to begin. She took a deep breath and explained her situation, how she had recently found out about the deception, and explained the story Grace had told her. Zac listened without interruption, nodding in places, and shaking his head in others, letting her pour it all out. When she finally came to a halt, he stepped in.

"Well, that explains a lot of things for me, things I never knew. Now I guess it's my turn to tell my side. After the night of the meeting with the two families, I was more or less under house arrest. We packed up pretty fast and moved to Salt Lake City. It broke my heart not to have a chance to say goodbye to Lucy.

"Once we got there, they continued to watch my every move, they drove me everywhere and waited until I went in to where I was supposed to go and were waiting for me when I came out. One of the first things they did was have a meeting with a few of the members of the Church, explaining my, umm, indiscretions, shall we say, and they all offered their support. I was enrolled into every church activity they could find and wherever I went, people kept an eye on me. My folks were determined I would re-establish myself in the Church, repent for my errors and reconnect with God, although to be honest, I never felt I had lost Him, despite my breach of the rules.

"One of the first things I did was write a long letter to Lucy, hoping to give it to one of my school friends to post for me, but my Dad spotted the bulge in my pocket before I even left the house. After that, they searched me every day. They checked up on me in my room all the time, and ensured I never had any money on me, so I couldn't even write to her at school then pay someone to buy envelopes and postage."

"Oh my gosh, that's horrendous, it sounds like you were a prisoner. Did you never try and stand up to them?"

"All the time at first. I argued with them that I loved Lucy, that there would never be anyone else and as soon as I turned twenty-one, I would go and be with her and they would never see me again."

"What did they say to that?"

"They scoffed, said it was just a crush and by that time, I would have forgotten all about her."

"I also tried to tell them that she was young and would be scared, that she needed me, and no matter what, I was the father of her baby and I wanted to be just that, a father, not just a sperm donor. They said I was too young to fulfill that role with any accomplishment, that the baby would need far more than I could ever give. My dad said he would take care of things financially, and he only told me much later that he had sent regular checks to Lucy, but none of them were ever cashed and he eventually gave up."

"I'm really sorry, but to be blunt, your parents sound awful. How can people like this be upstanding members of the church?"

"That's a pretty deep question, but the simple answer is they really thought what they were doing was for the best, and it took me a lot of years to see that. Yes, many of their actions were colored and distorted by shame and pride, and that was very wrong, but everybody makes mistakes or takes a wrong turn at some point.

"They should have trusted the church to show compassion, understanding and forgiveness, which they would have done, but they panicked and ran. After that, they had to stand by what they had chosen to do and enforce it; they had backed themselves into a corner.

"I don't think they're bad people; they were just misguided in this particular situation. They did keep tabs on things and fed me information that they thought might help their case. When they told me Lucy had moved in with Grace, they managed to convince me that was the best thing for her. She would have the support of her sister who was already a mom; the baby would get the best care from an experienced helper, and would want for nothing in the Carpenter household. It made sense and I'm ashamed to admit, I gave up trying to fight or find ways to contact her. I'm so sorry."

"Did you ever see your parents again?"

"Yes, once I got used to the idea that you and Lucy were happy without me, I made overtures to them and we reconciled. It wasn't long after that my mother died and a few years later my father, too. Now it's just you, Celeste, Jessie and me." That touched her troubled heart, and she smiled.

Courtney pondered over all she had learned, trying to put herself in his seventeen-year-old shoes. "You know, I guess I'm beginning to see the full picture of why everyone made the decisions they did and how it all led to where we all are today."

"I should have fought harder, tried harder. Losing you and Lucy is a heartache and burden of guilt I've carried all my life. I did come, as soon as I was twenty-one, just like I said I would.

"The first thing I found out was that Lucy had fallen in love, was happily married and that you had been adopted by your new dad. After a few sleepless nights in a cheap motel, I decided things were better left alone, that you were all better off without me. I was still a student, with a long way to go before I could offer stability and since Lucy seemed happy, I figured I had been a teenage crush for her. You had a new daddy and disrupting your new life just felt selfish. I packed up and headed back to Baltimore with my tail between my legs."

"I'm sorry to say it wasn't all that happy a marriage, and my dad wasn't the best influence in my life."

The pained expression that crossed Zac's face spoke volumes. "Thinking that you were both happy was the only thing that kept me going, the only way I could get on with my life."

They stared at each other, both their open faces revealing the same thought, *how different things could have been if life hadn't taken the turns it had.* After several moments of silence, Zac spoke again.

"I came to the funeral you know?"

"No I didn't, nobody told me."

"Nobody saw me, I hung around on the side-lines and no one noticed me amongst the hundreds that attended. It was a risk, because it certainly wasn't the right time to meet you, but I had to pay my respects."

"I'm glad," Courtney nodded, approving of the action. "So why did you never get in touch after that?"

"I never figured that you didn't know I was your father. I spent years hoping you would get in touch, but when you didn't, I assumed you just didn't want to know me. I get updates; I know you're Courtney Carpenter now, and a very accomplished young woman. Who was I to interfere or disrupt that?"

"My dad, that's who!"

Zac placed an arm around her shoulder and pulled her close. "Courtney, we've lost so much time, let's not waste another second. Would you like to meet your little sisters?"

Courtney pulled back and looked at Zac in surprise. "They know about me?"

"Yep, almost the minute I got your message. They're excited as all get out to have an older sister they can talk to about clothes, make-up, and boys. Girl stuff!"

"Well, then, what are we waiting for? I can't wait to meet them!"

Father and daughter smiled at each other, excited at the prospect of finally being a part of each other's lives.

Chapter Thirteen

Courtney felt absolutely on top of the world. The meeting with Zac and her sisters had gone really well. The two girls were young enough not to think too deeply about the situation, they were just keen to get to know this new member of their family. That gave Courtney pause for thought. At what point did people change from their childlike, easy acceptance of situations to overstressing, overthinking and worrying about everything?

She decided that while there were many things from childhood that were good to leave behind, there were actually a few things you should try to keep within your grasp. Taking things at face value and then finding the best in them were two of those.

The meeting hadn't been a long one this time. Zac needed to get the girls home to ensure they had done their homework and were in bed at a decent time for school the next day, but she had been invited over to their place the next Saturday, for pretty much the whole day. He had promised he would book the day off and hope he didn't get called in on an emergency, although he couldn't make any promises. The fact that he was willing to try was more than good enough for Courtney.

They probably still had many questions for each other, but their intense discussion had covered a lot of old ground and cleared away the past. The only place to go now was forward. She was determined that they would build a relationship and remain part of each other's lives from now on. She hadn't found him just to let him go again.

Peter had been waiting for her patiently, although he seemed a little anxious as she approached. When he saw her beaming face, she could see him visibly relax. The last few weeks had left her in no doubt that he cared about her deeply, but she would have to figure out at some point if he cared for her the same way as she cared for him.

She babbled about the visit the whole way home and he'd barely gotten a word in edgeways. He listened with his usual patience and supportiveness and told her how pleased he was for her. The embrace he gave her as he dropped her off back home made her tingle all over and was the fodder for many a daydream, but Courtney knew she needed to look deep inside herself before she faced that particular topic.

On arriving home, she found Grace and Cassie waiting for her in the family room and she gladly began the story over from the beginning, recounting every detail. Grace shed quite a few tears throughout as she learned of the fate of her baby sister's one true love. And Cassie being Cassie asked if she could write a story based loosely on the events in one of her books. Courtney went to bed on a high, excitement and happiness denying her sleep, as it did for the next two nights.

It was Wednesday now, and she was exhausted but still happy. She berated herself for not making much of a job of concentrating at work but her mind just wasn't able to settle recently. Making a decision, she picked up the phone and dialed an internal extension.

"Grace Carpenter's office, how may I help you?"

"Hi, it's Courtney, could you put me through please, Sandra?"

"Certainly, hold please."

"Grace Carpenter."

"Hi, it's me, Courtney. Listen, I'm having a hard time concentrating and I'm worried I'll do more harm than good being here. Is it okay if I just take off and count this as a vacation day?"

"Of course, there's nothing wrong is there?"

"No, no, nothing like that. I just have something on my mind that I need to think through."

"Okay, fine, just remember I'm here if you need to talk, or you could go get Cassie if you want some company."

"Thanks, I'll keep it in mind but I think this is something I have to figure out on my own."

"Good luck with it then, and have a nice day."

"Thanks."

Courtney replaced the phone, stepped out of her office, informed her assistant that she would be out for the rest of the day, and headed for her car. She wasn't sure where she was going but she figured home to change out of her business clothes would be a good start. Once back in her bedroom she hesitated, torn between hiking and riding. Deciding riding would take too much concentration, she pulled her thick hiking socks from the drawer and her boots from the closet.

Suitably dressed for her excursion, she headed to the kitchen to search out some goodies for her backpack. Maggie looked up and smiled as she entered.

"Not working today?"

"I went in for a couple of hours but had a change of heart; decided I needed to talk to the mountain today."

Maggie nodded, knowing exactly what Courtney meant. Hiking along the rugged trails connected you with nature, helping you find a more serene, instinctual, and primal way of being. It was a way of stripping back the layers of complexity human nature always added to every problem and allowed you to see more clearly. The mountain - stoic, ancient, and wise - was an expert listener who never offered inane opinions; just let you work things out for yourself.

"Want me to make you up a nice packed lunch?"

"Thanks, but I can do it, I can see you're already busy preparing something amazing for dinner. I'll try not to get in your way."

"You're never in the way, dear, you just dive right in."

As Courtney gathered the fixings for a sandwich, she looked thoughtfully at Maggie. "How difficult was it for Simone to rejoin the church?"

Maggie looked at Courtney sagely. "You're not referring to her own personal experience are you? You want to know about how other people took to the idea?"

"Yes."

"Most of them were really supportive and encouraging. If I had to sum it up, I would say she was welcomed back with open arms."

"Nobody judged her on her past?"

"I dare say there might have been a few that did, but they kept it to themselves. I think they're happy now that she has proven herself a worthy member. Most understand that it's easy to lose your way once in a while, and the church is there to help you find your way back, not push you away when you get close. You know, Courtney, we don't go to Church because we're perfect; we go because we're sinners hoping for perfection one day."

"Thanks, Maggie. That really helps."

Courtney, intent on her sandwich, missed Maggie's small, happy smile. With her backpack stuffed with food and bottles of water, she drove to a parking lot at the base of the mountain and set off on the trail. Being a midweek morning, there was hardly anyone in sight. After finding the rhythm of her stride, she let her mind roam over what she knew.

Fact #1: She was absolutely head over heels in love with Peter.

Fact #2: If she was to have any chance of a future with him, she needed to share his religion.

Those were undeniable. The only thing that was in doubt was whether she was worthy of either the church or Peter. Almost everyone in her close circle were members of the church, including her newly-discovered dad, and her two new little sisters were being raised as members of the church. Some of that group had made mistakes in their past, but they were forgiven for them and awarded second chances, not by the church itself but through the atonement of Jesus Christ. *Salvation! So that's what it means.*

If her mom hadn't married David Fisher, then Courtney would have been reared in the church at her mom's request, taken along by Grace and her family. Would that have been so bad? Maybe it would have given her a better way to deal with the loss of her mom, which hit her hard all over again when she reached her teens. She might not have turned to partying the way she did, but there was no way to tell.

Considering her own past, she decided that the things she'd done weren't so bad, some booze, the odd cigarette, coffee; no, those things she could forgive herself for, and if she could forgive herself, that was a good step toward being forgiven by God.

What I really need to atone for are all the times I raged against Him, ranting over the unfairness of life, berating my family for their unwavering belief and scoffing at their acceptance of any injustice that came their way.

During those angry years, their claims that things were part of God's plan for them had seemed like the lame excuses of someone who didn't have answers for why He allowed bad things to happen to good people.

Now, as she strode her way up the mountain trail, things were beginning to come together. It was as if her life decisions and actions were all connected with tiny silver threads, one leading to another, others entwined together. Trying to work her way back through each event that had led her to this point in her life was mind blowing, almost impossible.

It was far too twisted, she could go further and further back and things still connected, some in a line, others from tangled sidelines. *If it hadn't been for that, this wouldn't have happened; if that hadn't happened then I wouldn't have reacted by doing this.*

Her mind whirled with the complexity, and suddenly she felt very small, very insignificant. It would take a far greater mind than hers to pinpoint the exact thing that led her to this mountainside today.

She gasped and staggered, feeling dizzy. She stopped to steady herself, floored by the almost cosmic revelation that had just hit her. She couldn't do it because it wasn't for her to do.

Yes, of course she had free will to make choices, but those choices had arisen from things that had been placed in her path, gotten in the way of her carefully worked out, straight-line plan for her life. And that plan had been developed by the person she had become after all that had gone before.

I had to go through it, for whatever reasons, to make me who I am today. The statement brought comfort, and she suddenly had a feeling that she was meant to be here, right here and right now, and that she wasn't alone.

It unnerved her and she looked around anxiously. *Oh, my gosh! I've been walking for hours, far too lost in thought to pay much attention except to ensure the trail was still beneath my feet. I shouldn't climb any higher without the added safety of the climbing gear I left behind in my walk-in closet.*

She couldn't see anything to account for the feeling of being accompanied, and when her stomach growled, she decided to throw down her rug and have something to eat and drink before turning back. It would be silly to risk collapsing through dehydration halfway down the trail.

Judging by the sun, it must be around late afternoon, maybe as late as early evening. There's plenty of daylight left; no need to dig out my cell phone just to check the time.

As she ate and drank, Courtney felt more settled than she had in a long time. Her mind that had been in a turmoil for weeks was finally quiet, the decision made. Contented and at peace, she lay down on the blanket to soak in the last of the sun's warmth.

Chapter Fourteen

The lonely, haunting hoots of an owl woke Courtney from her sleep. The insomnia-filled nights she experienced lately had finally caught up with her and, lying on the blanket, warmed by the sun in this stunning setting, she had been lulled into a blissful doze, leading to a deep, dreamless slumber. Berating herself for her stupidity, she dug in her pack for her phone, startled when she realized it was after midnight.

Unwilling to be disturbed today, she had turned her phone to silent, and the amount of missed calls and messages informed her that her family were frantic with worry at her lack of communication. Fingers flying over the illuminated screen, Courtney texted Grace. The message was simple, everything was fine and she'd be home in a few hours. She neglected to mention that she was still practically at the summit of Mt. Timpanogos. Rooting around in her backpack, she was disgusted at herself for leaving behind the large, heavy flashlight that was part of her kit. She'd taken out anything she had felt she wouldn't need but would add bulk and weight to the pack.

She took a few deep breaths and looked around. The night was clear, the sky filled with a million twinkling stars and the moon was almost full. She was certain there was more than enough natural light to safely hike back down the trail. What she didn't have was anything for protection against possible wildlife encounters. Bear sightings were rare here, but she knew they did exist, along with the mountain lions and cougars that were reported to make their homes high up in the mountain.

Keeping her head, she told herself that the reported evidence of these was so flimsy that it was unlikely she was going to be the one to stumble across them tonight. She was far more at risk from the herds of moose that were used to humans and decidedly unafraid of them. If they were startled, they could be very aggressive. She really didn't want to fight with a large, territorial bull or an angry mama protecting her little ones.

Gathering up her things, she felt that sense of being accompanied again and instead of making her feel uneasy, this time it comforted her and soothed her. *Is this what Peter refers to as 'feeling the Spirit?'* Now she knew she would be just fine on her night-time hike. This afternoon, she had accepted the full truth of God in all His glory, reached out to Him to accept her as His pupil, His follower, His daughter. In return, He had reached out to her, accepting her willingly into His fold. She would surefootedly walk this path with confidence, because it was His path. He had brought her here and He would lead her home.

She set off, but after only a few steps she hesitated, tilting her head to better hear something that caught her attention, probably an animal of some sort. A faint cry in the night, indecipherable at first. She strained her ears harder, and yes, she could finally make it out.

"Courrrrrrrt-ney! Courrrrrrrt-ney! Can you hear me?"

She almost laughed aloud when she recognized the voice. *My Peter has come to save me as always, perhaps sent to save me.* Maggie was the only one who knew she was hiking, and she hadn't told her which trail she was going to use.

Had Peter been up and down them all, finally getting lucky, or had he been guided to her, open as he was to the gentle push from a powerful hand? She was overwhelmed by the desire to ask him, to talk to him, to rejoice in her newfound discoveries.

She peered into the darkness below and saw the tiny bob of a flashlight in the distance. He was on the right trail, just as she had known he would be.

"Peter, I'm here, I'm on my way down," she called and began to make her way carefully down the trail.

As the light came closer, it danced erratically and she could hear the crunch of Peter's running feet in his desperation to reach her. Three quarters of the way up the trail to the summit of Mt. Timpanogos, Peter reached her, dropped his flashlight and scooped her up into his arms, almost crushing her in his relief.

"You're safe! Oh thank God you're safe."

Courtney flung back her head and laughed as Peter spun her around in his glee. "I'm fine Peter; I'm better than fine."

He placed the dizzy Courtney back on the ground but seemed reluctant to allow her free of his grasp. "What did you think you were doing, staying up here until this time of night? Everyone's been worried sick. If it hadn't been for my dad organizing a search party, Grace would have been up here herself and probably called in the National Guard by now."

"I'm sorry, I stopped to eat and fell asleep. I feel like a rookie idiot."

"As long as you're alright, nothing else matters."

"Are there a lot of people out looking? Have I caused a lot of trouble?"

"Some, yeah, but isn't that your specialty?"

"Hey, I don't do it on purpose!"

"I know; it's a natural talent. My dad's out with Jimmy Taylor, Brett Sutcliffe, Ian Johnson and a few others. They were sure you'd be on the Timpanogos loop hike so they were spreading out around that, but I just had a feeling you'd be on the Timpooneke Trail."

Despite being desperately sorry for the worry and trouble she had caused all these amazing people who had rallied round to help, Courtney couldn't stop the grin that spread from ear to ear. "I just knew you'd been sent to find me."

Peter looked down at her quizzically under the playful light of the moon. "You did?"

"I did," she said. "Please call your dad and tell him thank you so much, but you've found me and everyone can go home.

I'll call them all personally in the morning to extend my own thanks."

Reluctantly Peter let go of her and made the call. Once he'd hung up, Courtney sidled up to him and slid her arm through his. "Can I ask you something?"

"Of course."

They walked in step, arm-and-arm down the narrow trail. "If a girl decided she wanted, no, *needed* to join the Church, would you be willing, and allowed, to be her teacher, even though you're not a missionary anymore?"

Peter stopped walking and turned Courtney to face him, his hands firmly on her shoulders. His expression said he dared not hope that she was asking what he thought she was asking. "Would this girl be a former snot-nosed, gangly tear away that I've known since she was seven-years-old?"

"She might be," Courtney replied with an impish grin.

Peter's smoky eyes practically glowed with joy. "Then I'm sure I could obtain permission from the church and the backing of her family to carry out the lessons."

Courtney swallowed hard before she formed the next question. "And if perhaps you … um … maybe wanted to date this girl, would that be completely unethical and against the rules?"

"Would this girl be interested in dating me?"

"Next to becoming a member of the Church, it would the most important thing in this girl's life."

Peters' face spread into a slow, easy smile. "Then I'm sure it could be worked out."

Under the smiling moon and a million dancing stars, Peter pulled Courtney to him and kissed her, a long slow tender kiss that whispered of a lifetime and beyond in his arms, a kiss that spoke to more than her body, it reached directly into her very soul and completed her.

As they pulled apart, she gasped. "Peter, I love you."

She immediately felt embarrassed, blurting it out that way, but she couldn't help it. She had kept it to herself for far too long and they were words that wanted to be shouted from every rooftop with glee. Still, they hadn't even had a first date yet and here she was, dropping the L-bomb on him like an infatuated teenager. "I'm sorry, I shouldn't have said that."

Peter stroked the back of her head softly. "Why not, I've said it to you a million times."

"Yeah, but like, in the friend way."

Peter threw his head back and laughed. "Seriously, you never knew? Courtney, I was your friend for about a week while I got to know you. From that moment on, I knew you were the girl for me. I told myself it was childhood infatuation, then a teenage crush, but as I matured, I knew it was the real thing. It has always been you Courtney, and will always be you. If I couldn't have you, then I'd be content as a bachelor for the rest of my days."

"Are you saying what I think you're saying?"

"I'm saying I'm in love with you, madly, passionately and wildly in love."

"Me, too," Courtney had time to reply before they came together for another kiss, inflamed with passion but just as beautiful as the first. As they broke the connection, they stared into each other's eyes with wonder, Peter stroking her hair.

"We really should get off this mountain," Peter said.

"We should," Courtney affirmed, neither of them moving. Another stolen, moonlit kiss later, they finally began to walk, arms entwined around one another.

"You know what," Peter said conversationally as they matched their steps. "If it wasn't for teaching you what you need to know about the gospel and a year wait, I'd ask you to marry me right away. Every day we've spent together has felt like a date, we must be at least at the hundred mark by now."

Courtney giggled. "We must be. I would accept, but I'm also looking forward to all the dating we'll get to do while you're teaching me the gospel. The anticipation will make it even better. You have a lot to teach me beforehand, but I bet I have a lot to teach you afterwards."

Peter groaned. "Why do I have the feeling that these lessons might have to be supervised?"

"Because according to Officer Bradshaw, I'm nothing but a wanton temptress, remember?"

"Oh, I remember alright, and I have to agree, but in the near future, you're going to be *my* wanton temptress."

"Hey, I just had a thought."

"Hmm?"

"If I was the only one for you, and if I hadn't decided I wanted to join the Church, and you stayed a bachelor, does that mean you would have died a *virgin*?"

Peter shook his head, knowing he was going to have his work cut out for him. Teaching Courtney was probably going to be the hardest but most rewarding thing he had ever done, even compared to the resistance he had sometimes encountered as a missionary. "Yes, Courtney, I would have died a virgin."

"Man, that would have been rough, but you know what? I probably would have too. Now how sad is that!"

"You never wanted anyone else either?"

"Nope, never."

"Then I don't think it's sad, I think it's beautiful."

"I guess it is."

"Just as well we both trusted in God enough to know that he wouldn't let that happen, that he'd bring us to each other eventually, the way it was always meant to be."

"We could have saved a lot of time and been married by now. If Mom hadn't met David Fisher, I'd have been brought up in the church like she wanted."

"It obviously wasn't meant to happen that way; you had to make this decision for yourself; that's how He wanted it."

Courtney nodded, the truth and clarity of the words obvious to her now. She still had a lot to learn, but these last few months had brought her a long way toward a deep understanding of salvation and how this whole thing worked. She was fascinated and awed by it, and couldn't wait to explore it further, to truly understand how God and Jesus Christ have loved her all long.

Hoping to lighten the mood for now, she looked cheekily up at Peter. "Who'd have thought God would be looking after my sex life, too? That's pretty awesome."

"Courtney Carpenter, I have absolutely no idea what I am going to do with you! It's just as well I'm going to be a big part of your life to keep you on the straight and narrow."

Courtney giggled. "I love you, Peter Anderson."

"And I love you, Courtney Carpenter."

"Just don't ever stop."

"I won't, we're together for eternity."

"Just what I've been hoping for!"

They walked the rest of the way in silence, arms wrapped around each other, surrounded by the glorious handiwork of their Creator. As they reached their cars in the lot, they kissed once more and parted reluctantly. Driving away separately, they knew that with the new dawn would come a new life, a brand new beginning, a beginning that would lead to the union of their lives and their souls for a lifetime and beyond.

Will Courtney and Peter get married? How does Carter's new love interest, Kate, turn the entire Carpenter clan upside down? You'll find the answers in Book 4!

Coming May, 2016

Survival - Carter's Story
A Christian Romance

The Carpenter Chronicles, Book 4

Here's an excerpt from Survival – Carter's Story:

As he approached, Carter saw he was in luck, only two of the six tables were occupied. About to claim his space, he was disconcerted to hear the sounds of sniffling from the next table. He glanced over, seeing a young woman with her head bowed over the table and a large handkerchief covering her face.

Most men might have found the sight of a crying woman uncomfortable and awkward and avoided it at all costs, but Carter wasn't most guys. Growing up in a houseful of females, he was no stranger to tears and his instincts to comfort and protect were instantly triggered. He walked the few small steps to her table.

"Excuse me, are you alright?"

"Perfectly fine, I always sit in cafes and cry."

The voice was muffled from behind the handkerchief and Carter resisted the urge to chuckle at the sarcasm, knowing it would anger her. She hadn't meant to be funny. "Okay, let me rephrase the question. Is there anything I can do to make whatever the situation is better for you?"

The woman raised her head and looked up at Carter with red-rimmed eyes. Recognition flooded his brain as he saw her face for the first time. "Katherine? Katherine Jameson?"

"Peterson, Katherine Peterson now," she answered robotically, as if on autopilot. Suddenly, her expression changed. "Holy smoke, Carter Carpenter! What are you doing in San Francisco?"

"I live and work here now. Mind if I take a seat?"

"Oh, where are my manners, please do. I'm so sorry; I'm all over the place right now."

Carter sat down opposite Katherine, marveling at the chance encounter. He'd met her during the undergraduate architectural program at California Polytechnic State University in San Luis Obispo. She had been the long-term girlfriend of his roommate, Joshua Peterson, and therefore, he'd gotten to know her pretty well. She was around most of the time and they had often double dated or gone out with just the three of them. When he'd moved on to Colombia for his graduate program, he'd initially made an effort to keep in touch with Joshua and Katherine, but as so often happens, life had taken over and contact trailed off.

"So since I'm an old friend and not some random stranger, will you tell me what's wrong?"

"Carter, I wouldn't even know where to start, everything's wrong. I take it you heard about Joshua?"

Carter frowned. "No, last contact I had was an invitation to your engagement party, but I was in the middle of finals and couldn't come. How is he?"

Katherine started crying again. "He's dead, Carter. Joshua is dead."

Carter's face went pale. He and Josh were the same age, they'd been roommates and great friends. How could he possibly be dead so young? What on earth had happened? Instead of bombarding her with questions, Carter scooted his chair around so he could place a comforting arm around her shoulders. He gently rubbed her back as she sobbed, waiting for her to cry herself out. It always happened eventually; he knew from experience that patience and understanding was the best he could offer right now. As her sobs turned to sniffles, she wiped at her eyes with the oversized handkerchief again.

"I'm sorry, I'm a mess. You must be embarrassed to be sitting here with me like this." She glanced around to see if someone was watching them.

"Not at all, and you have nothing to apologize for. I do think you need to talk about this though. I think you've been bottling everything up."

"There isn't anyone I can talk to about everything that's going on."

"There's me," he offered.

Register to Get Your Pre-Order Copy Here

In Case You Missed Book Two!

Best Seller
Sanctuary, Chelsea's Story
The Carpenter Chronicles, Book Two

Available now in paperback and ebook.

Click here to order book two of the series.

In Case You Missed Book One!

Best Seller
Sacrifice, Carrie's Story
The Carpenter Chronicles, Book One

Available now in paperback and ebook.

Click here to order book one of the series.

If you've enjoyed reading this book, I'd like to ask a favor of you. Will you please leave some positive feedback on the Amazon sales page for it so other readers will know you liked it. It will really help get our Christian message out and I would so, so appreciate it.

Just click here!

For updates on coming releases, and discount pricing for books by
Janice Limb Myers,
please sign up here:

http://JaniceLimbMyers.com

Support Christian Authors and Read Great Books:
Christian Books in Multiple Genres, Join Christian Indie Author
~ Readers Group on Facebook for opportunities to learn about more
great Christian authors.
https://www.facebook.com/groups/291215317668431/